Praise for Ann Vremont's *Reluctant Muse*

Gold Star Review

"Beautiful, amazing and fabulous .... the *Reluctant Muse* is an incredible book. Ms. Vremont has a total grasp on her craft .... This book flowed seamlessly, with wonderful characters and a beautiful love story."

~ Marcy Arbitman, Just Erotic Romance Reviews

Five Flags

"*Reluctant Muse* lives up to every bit of its promise! This is a wonderful story which brings hope to every reader (and reviewer) who doesn't quite fit the perfect model heroine ... Kudos to Ann Vremont..."

~ Annie, Euro-Reviews

Four and a Half Stars

"*Reluctant Muse* has to be one of the most passionate and tender stories I have read in a long time. With a perfect blend of humor, charm and passion this is a must read from beginning to end."

~ Kimberly Spinney, Ecataroman~~~ (Sen~~~al)

Reluctant Muse

Ann Vremont

A Samhain Publishing, Ltd. publication.

Samhain Publishing, Ltd.
512 Forest Lake Drive
Warner Robins, GA 31093
www.samhainpublishing.com

Reluctant Muse
Copyright © 2006 by Ann Vremont
Print ISBN: 1-59998-391-5
Digital ISBN: 1-59998-154-8

Editing by Jewell Mason
Cover by Anne Cain

First Samhain Publishing, Ltd. electronic publication: October 2006
First Samhain Publishing, Ltd. print publication: April 2007

Dedication

Boo

Chapter One

The knock on Bryce Schoene's front door sounded tentative, as if the visitor questioned whether it was the right apartment. Bryce's gaze dropped to the bottom right corner of her laptop's screen where the time showed a few minutes before five o'clock. Squaring her shoulders, she focused on the blank Word file in front of her. It was Friday and—graduate degree hanging in the balance—she had a paper due Monday. She decided to ignore the knocking. Ninety to one odds, it was a stranger confused by the ambiguously numbered apartments.

She sorted through the jumble of ideas she had brainstormed on the bus ride home from campus, their previous brilliance extinguished by further thought. The knock came again, more assured this time, and Bryce chewed at her bottom lip. She considered starting the story with a knock on the door. But who would be on the other side, and why?

The visitor spoke on the third round of knocking, both the words and raps coming sharp and fast. "I can hear you thinking in there. Open up!"

The odd choice of words broke her concentration.

Hear me thinking?

Bryce swiveled the office chair until she faced the door. Despite the heavy muffle of oak, she could tell the visitor was a woman, the voice feminine and totally unfamiliar.

"Yes, I said 'thinking'. Open the door, Bryce," the woman called again. "I certainly don't have all weekend to stand around."

She knows my name? The chair groaned in protest as Bryce rose, and she winced. She walked quietly to the door, hoping the visitor was only bluffing and hadn't heard the chair's squeak.

"Come on, doll baby, this won't take long."

Despite the endearment, the woman didn't sound anything other than persistent—and likely to draw a crowd from among the many nosy neighbors whose apartments ringed the building's courtyard. Just imagining a week or more worth of curious looks from her neighbors made Bryce's skin crawl.

Approaching the door from the side, she reached up and slid the chain lock into place. Then she undid the top two deadbolts and slowly turned the doorknob. Nervous energy ran through her hand and arm, and it took her a few seconds to realize she had opened the door as wide as the chain allowed.

The two inch slice of open door revealed a petite blonde, with powder blue eyes and a slash of killer red lipstick slickening her wide mouth. Except for the peek of black boots from beneath her pants, red leather hugged her slim frame. The material's shade, slightly darker than the lipstick, dipped toward a dried crimson. She looked, Bryce thought, like she'd just finished a shift on the corner of *Hooker and Vine.*

"'Hooker and Vine?' Is this how you start all job interviews?" the woman asked.

Bryce jerked back from the door, and her brows knitted together over whether she'd actually voiced the insult. The question was abruptly pushed out of mind as the woman's second question sank in.

"Job interview?" Bryce asked. It sounded like a sales pitch. Dressed like she was, the woman definitely had *something* to sell. Bryce put her palm flat on the door and started to push, but the blonde wedged her black-booted foot between the door and its frame.

Oh, hell, no. She just didn't. Did she?

Bryce cocked an eyebrow at the woman and slowly raised her bare foot, threatening to place it against the blonde's twig of a leg. The woman sighed at the threat, the air leaving her in a long curling manner like spirals of smoke from a half-chewed cigar.

Like spirals of smoke...what the fuck?

"You'll get used to it," the blonde smiled. "And if you don't, it's just for the weekend."

"Lady..." Bryce began and looked around for something else to force the woman's foot back through the door, "I don't know what you're talking about, but you've got the wrong Bryce. Okay?"

"No, doll baby." Her smile pulled the already wide mouth into a broad, thin line of determination. "Bryce Schoene, right? Bryce the Beautiful."

Bryce the Beautiful. Well, that proved it—no one had ever called her beautiful.

"Lady, you've definitely got the wrong Bryce."

Red-tipped fingers reached through the door and wrapped around the safety chain. The air surrounding the woman's fist vibrated like a hummingbird's wings and then the chain snapped. She swept past the stunned Bryce and into the room's center before glancing at her watch.

"It's almost eight-fifteen in New York, doll baby," she said. She gave a casual flick of her wrist and the watch slid beneath the sleeve of her red leather jacket just as the apartment door slammed shut. "So here's the quick and dirty version, alrighty?"

Bryce put her hand up, hoping the "stop" motion seemed both calm and in command. "Why don't we discuss this out in the courtyard, La...Miss?"

The darker ash blonde of the woman's manicured eyebrows shot halfway up her forehead, and she held one slim hand in front of her mouth, just far enough away to avoid smudging her lipstick. The giggle she seemed to be fighting back escaped and she dropped the hand to clutch at her stomach. The laugh only grew in volume. "First, I'm in your head, so don't waste time trying to trick me into the courtyard or anywhere else. Second, you can call me Percy for now."

"Percy...well, that's a start, I guess—"

"A damn slow one," Percy interrupted. "Now where's the uniform? You have to wear it, you know, for this to work."

Bryce stared at her for a moment. *A joke.* It had to be a joke, even if she couldn't think of anyone who would bother to play one on her. *Or maybe it was some new television show? Had the L.A. producers actually stooped so low they were invading people's homes now?*

While Bryce's mind raced through the possibilities, Percy's hand looped circles in the air, her whole body conveying the need to speed things up. "Right, okay. A TV show. That sounds good." The words came out rapid fire as Percy scanned the room. "But shows need costumes, right? I know I sent it ahead—so where did you put it?"

Had Bryce just mentioned the possibility of a show out loud? "Put wh—"

"A-ha! Gotcha!" Percy headed in a straight line for the computer chair where a tall package waited wrapped in cream-colored tissue paper and tied off with a crimson ribbon.

The paper rustled when Percy lifted it from the chair. Spinning on the heels of her shiny black boots, she presented it to Bryce with a curtsy. "If you'd be so kind as to strip and put this on?"

She waited while Bryce stared open-mouthed. With an exaggerated sigh, she offered the package a second time.

"I...w-was just...sit-sitting...there." The protest left her in a slow and broken string of words as Bryce tried to account for how Percy could have not only hidden the bulky package beneath the tight leather jacket and pants, but also removed it noiselessly and placed it on the chair some six feet away. Even now the paper made a whispered crackle as Percy held it forward.

"Yeah, the seat's still warm," she answered, another giggle threatening to bust loose. "Now, are you going to put it on, or do I have to do that, too?"

Asking the question, Percy plucked the ribbon's knot loose and let it fall to the floor along with the tissue paper. In her hand remained a charm bracelet and a dazzling white bundle of linen.

"It's an amulet chain," Percy sighed out and held it up. "Not a 'charm bracelet'." She plucked through the small figures. "Silver and gold laced together for the chain. Pegasus in ivory, a skull in, well, bone, of course." Fingering past more figures, she held up an ass carved in brown agate and a gryphon in topaz. "My favorites, but you don't need to worry about what's on it. So long as it's on you—and you're wearing the sheet."

"Look, I'm not finding this funny." Bryce backed toward the door, one hand searching for the doorknob, the other ready to swipe at Percy if she decided to charge. *Man, does L.A. have its whack jobs.* "It isn't at all amusing."

"But it is a-*musing*," Percy answered.

A glow that Bryce would have readily characterized as insane lit the woman's gaze, and the smile she wore stretched her mouth to a point that convinced Bryce this nutcase meant to swallow her whole.

"In fact," Percy continued pressing. "A-*musing* we will go...well, just you, actually. Me, I haven't had a vacation since Chaucer died. And you're helping me get one this weekend, whether you want to or not, doll baby."

Raising the charm bracelet in one hand, she let the linen partially unfold to the floor. It was a single swath of fabric that looked over a dozen feet long. She gave the bracelet a shake and the linen turned into a pair of jeans and a UCLA school sweatshirt.

My UCLA sweatshirt! Bryce froze in her backward retreat. The chill of the apartment's air conditioning made the hair on her suddenly bare arms stand up. The linen draped her body, curling and knotting around her. She looked at Percy, and then shut her eyes when the woman's blonde hair ran long and green. Starbursts patterned Bryce's closed eyelids in a psychedelic strobe and she forced her eyes back open. Percy stalked her, now looking as if someone had drawn her in the dark outline of an uncolored comic. She held the charm bracelet in front of her as she moved, her attempts to catch one of Bryce's wrists unsuccessful.

"Stay still!" Percy issued her command with a growl that sounded more like a plea. "There's only one rule to being a muse—you have to wear the damn uniform. *All* of it." She let out a frustrated trill as Bryce dodged her again. "And you have to *accept* this."

At five-four, Percy stood about half a foot shorter than Bryce and looked like she weighed at least a hundred pounds less. Ignoring the size difference, Percy pounced on her. Thighs locked tight against Bryce's hips and waist, she wrapped an arm around the back of Bryce's neck. The shift in weight spun Bryce around, her arms frantically wind-milling for something to grab and coming up empty. Bryce fell onto the couch. Her wrist bounced off the wooden armrest. Pain shot through the bone and she pulled her hand to her chest.

Percy snapped the bracelet around Bryce's other wrist and gave a triumphant "woot". "There! Bracelet accepted."

The sound of voices, dozens of them, joined the wildly dancing colors already infecting Bryce's vision. Percy's voice cut through the growing din, but the blonde offered only a lame excuse for the havoc the fabric and amulet wreaked in Bryce's mind.

"What were you going to do all weekend, anyway? Stare at a blank computer screen?"

🁢 🁢 🁢

All of it.

All of it!

Percy's caveat repeated itself, somehow wriggling past the noise booming in Bryce's head. If she could just get the outfit and bracelet off, it should stop. She clawed at the chain. The clasp refused to yield to her fumbling fingers. Momentarily abandoning her attack on the chain, she pulled at the sheet. The more she strained to pull it off, the tighter the fabric clung to her body.

"Percy! Stop this! It's not funny." Realizing the woman had vanished even more abruptly than she had appeared, Bryce dropped to her knees and then to her hands as image melded to sound, sound to sight, the stimuli stacking themselves higher, pressing her down until she thought her spine would snap.

Through the soft pastels of a Monet landscape, she saw the hard glint of metal pruning shears on the other side of the patio's glass door. She pushed up and staggered forward, her softly voiced "thank you" as she found the door unlocked lost in the cacophony of invisible instruments battering her ear drums.

Bryce brought the shears up to where the linen wound over her shoulder. Her skin crawled with the itch of imaginary fire ants, and she tumbled through the potted rose bushes separating her patio from the neighboring one. She landed on her bottom as the shears sliced through the fabric. She grabbed the material at her waist, holding it as she scooted backward.

Once she was completely out of the sheet, her vision cleared and the time-etched granite beneath her faded to the patio's everyday concrete.

Sound still clawed at her, and she jammed one of the blades between her wrist and the chain. Twisting the shears, the chain snapped. The world went quiet—as if someone had shut off a giant faucet. The only sounds left were the erratic beat of her heart and the ragged pull of oxygen through her lungs.

And a very masculine voice—one she would recognize anywhere.

"Bryce? Are...are you okay?"

Chapter Two

Jeez-oh-Pete, please tell me I'm not sitting bare-assed on G. Diaz's patio.

Resisting the impulse to close her eyes and scrabble madly back through the rose bushes to her own patio, Bryce slowly turned and looked over her shoulder at the question's source. What she saw temporarily pushed everything else from her mind, even her own naked state.

Diaz was sitting on a stool, an easel in front of him. At his feet, he had dropped a paintbrush and the splatter of dark blue marked the surrounding concrete. It was August and hot. He was shirtless and barefoot, his muscled frame covered only in a loose pair of cotton shorts. Lighter in skin tone than most of the Latinos in the neighborhood, he nonetheless had a summer tan—the day's humidity turning his skin to a slicked bronze.

For a second, she let her gaze soak in the ripples of muscle that played over his abs before the skin smoothed like worked steel across his chest. She felt her nipples pebble, and the reality that she was naked and on his patio slammed into her once again.

Bryce scrambled to cover herself with the damaged piece of cloth. At the fabric's first touch against her skin, her vision began to blur and she tossed the sheet away. Audience or no audience, she couldn't put that thing back on. Wearing it had been like one of the bad acid trips her mother used to describe.

"Bryce, are you okay?" Shock wearing off, Diaz rose from the stool and repeated his question. Instead of scooping the sheet back up and offering it to Bryce, he dropped to his knees behind her and lightly touched her shoulder.

She was naked, and he was all but naked. They were poised there, him touching her, their bodies covered in moisture from the heat. Hadn't she dreamt this at least a couple dozen times since he had moved in at the beginning of the year? Hell, she'd fantasized about it while wide awake, with her fingers dizzily working her clit until she came quietly calling his name.

Of course, it could never be like I imagined it.

Giving a panicked snort, she turned her head forward and drew her legs up to her chest. "I need something to put on...please."

Diaz reached for the two halves of linen.

"Not that!" Seeing him freeze, she hastily added, "Allergies."

He picked up the fabric and turned until he was sitting facing her. "It's a flax linen, Bryce," he said, his expression incredulous.

"Uhm...I guess. So?" How the hell did he know her name, anyway? She couldn't remember telling him, only knew that her "B. Schoene" sat alongside his "G. Diaz" on the row of mailboxes at the front of the converted apartment building.

Beyond that, she'd essentially fled his unilateral attempts at conversation.

"Your blue shirt...the one you like to pair with the black pantsuit. That's linen, isn't it?"

Sensing her jaw was starting to drop, she buried her chin against her knees and clasped her arms tighter around her legs. She could feel flesh bulging, wet skin sliding against wet skin in the summer heat of L.A. Nothing ever bulged in the magazine or television ads. Nothing was wet and slippery unless the photographer wanted it that way. And just what the hell was he doing noticing her clothes like that or knowing what the hell flax linen was? Did he have a linen fetish?

"It's a different mix," she stammered. "Or maybe the metal." She inclined her head in the charm bracelet's direction.

Diaz scooted until his back rested against the patio door and he could see all of her at once. He tilted his head, first to the left, then to the right. His gaze seemed to draw a frame around her, reminding her of the easel just a few feet away.

Bryce hugged her knees tighter, trying to make herself smaller, invisible. Dressed, she had perfected the art of being invisible. With the right cut of clothing, a man's

19

attention skipped over her, registering neither lust nor disgust. The same idea applied to makeup. She always left the house with a light touch of color—enough for a professional appearance, but not so much she risked comments on her pretty face while the ugly caveat of her body went unvoiced but hanging in the air.

Naked, invisible wasn't an option.

He was still staring at her, running one half of the sheet through his hands like rosary beads. "I almost think you want to be naked on my patio, Bryce."

With a body and face like his, naked women falling over Diaz wouldn't surprise her. Still, he could hardly expect that to be *her* modus operandi for picking up men. She raised her head, gaze widening in challenge. "Naked on your patio is the last thing I want." In fact, she was going to have to find a new apartment now. There was no way she could keep passing him in the courtyard. His quiet, thoughtful gaze and the unusual ease it sometimes produced in her would be gone—from now on, she'd only see his stunned expression from finding her naked on his patio.

"Okay." He held the sheet out to her with his own challenge. His mouth tilted at the corners, the grin sensuous and surprisingly hungry.

"I-I told you. I can't put it on." Afraid to expose more of her body to his view, Bryce reined in the impulse to reach out and push the fabric away.

"Allergies, right?"

When she nodded, Diaz dropped the material to the concrete and scooted forward until he was close enough to run a finger down the side of her arm. The thin film of sweat covering her skin parted at his touch and ran in rivulets, as if she were melting from the contact. But then the warm melt turned to a sharp sting. She jerked her shoulder forward and looked at one of the superficial bloodied marks the rose bushes had scratched into the back of her arm when she fell through to the patio.

"Now...I see a few scrapes..." He paused, moving close enough to her that one shin was positioned along her side while his other leg rested warm and moist against her back. "But nothing like a rash."

Hell, he was practically cradling her with his lower body. *If he so much as lifted an arm...*

He smoothed his palm across the unmarked plane of her shoulder blade. "In fact, it's all very soft and cream colored." Keeping his arm bent, he ran his hand all the way across her back to her other shoulder. The motion brought his lips to within only a few millimeters of her ear. "No signs of swelling, either. Are you sure you're—"

"It's not like you could tell, really." *And there most certainly was swelling,* she thought as she inched away from him. Her clit was swollen, almost twitching with the need to be stroked. Why the hell was he tormenting her like this? He'd always seemed kind, never cruel, in their all too brief encounters. But now it seemed as if he were trying to seduce her and that could only be a joke on his part.

"Could you just get something, please...a robe maybe?" She didn't mean to snap the words out, but she did. Her tone pushed him a little farther away.

He slid closer to the building and then leaned back, his stomach muscles flexing as he reached up and opened the patio door. Watching Bryce watching him, Diaz patted blindly behind him.

Shit, why doesn't he just go inside—then I could run back through the bushes.

As if he had read her mind, Diaz lightly kicked the sheet and bracelet out of her reach. "Don't go anywhere," he said, rising quickly and stepping inside his apartment.

He stopped just inside the patio door, his head and torso hidden as he leaned over and rummaged through something just out of view.

Damn, he's got a nice ass. The thighs and glutes were thickly muscled, like a climber's or cyclist's powerful lower body. She knew he had a weight bench inside, had even sat against her wall reading to the sound of him working out. Sometimes, though, she had to carry the book into her bedroom, the sound of all that masculine grunting as he pumped weights—well, it had its own special effect. As often as not she let the book drop to the floor, hands roaming her body while she imagined all that noise was for her benefit.

Tilting her head, Bryce leaned forward as Diaz pulled a laundry basket closer to him and more of his mouth-watering lower torso came into view. She traced the curving lines of his legs, starting at the backward sweep of his calf and up over the front thigh with its medium dusting of black hair. Gaze traveling higher, surprise widened her expression.

He hadn't, had he? Popped wood...talking to her? While she was naked? If anything, things should have taken refuge higher up.

She relaxed the death grip she had on her knees and pried her attention from his erection to look at the discarded fabric, then at the easel Diaz had been sitting in front of when she'd stumbled onto his patio. She had learned, in part through her own casual observations when he'd moved in, but mostly from unwanted conversations with the nosy Mrs. Gretz across the way, that he worked as a professional artist producing commissioned portraits. She'd even asked him about it later in an exchange of neighborly pleasantries she hadn't otherwise managed to avoid. She tried to remember if he'd told her his name then. Had she been so petrified that she'd blanked on his name? All she could remember was that he suffered through the portraits to pay the rent while he waited for his other work to "catch on".

Which makes him a serious artist.

She thought of the hallucinations that had lasted until she had stripped the linen and chain away. And then there was Percy's outrageous behavior—the woman had pretty much stated that she was a muse and that Bryce was taking her place for the weekend. But Percy was a nutcase.

Or was she? Could all that male arousal be the product of one sliced up sheet and broken charm bracelet?

"I've wanted to paint you for months, but you never stop outside your apartment long enough to start a real conversation."

He was standing on the patio's threshold, a red and black kimono pressed against his lower abdomen. Bryce had a moment to wonder if he was still hard before she looked up to find him staring at her chest. She followed his gaze and realized she had dropped the protective shield of her arm while looking at the easel. Her breasts were fully exposed, as was her arousal. Her nipples were drawn tight, the areolas darkened in excitement from pale cherry to a deep red.

Diaz blinked once, slowly, his hand jerking against the kimono and what had grown to an only partially concealed erection. He pulled his lower lip into his mouth, licking it as he did so.

"To paint you like this."

Bryce remained motionless. This really couldn't be happening. Not the Percy thing, not sitting naked in front of Diaz with his body responding as if the sight of her was turning him on. She swallowed, her throat parched at the same time her mouth salivated over the outline of his ample cock pressed hard against a formerly loose pair of cotton shorts.

"Will you let me paint you?"

Soft and low, the question had all the sexual power of a full-throated purr. Bryce's mouth twitched with the perverse desire to tell Diaz he could paint her white if he wanted to. She didn't think it was possible for her nipples to get any tighter, but the idea of his coming—on her or in her—sent her body temperature spiking higher. Far from wanting to run, her initial response was to fully unfold in front of him. Maybe if the whole Percy thing was real, so was this.

No, Percy was a whack job—an infectious one at that if Bryce was starting to believe there was any possibility that she really had been deputized by a runaway muse or that Diaz found her body inspiring.

"Bryce." He whispered her name, a slight tremble running through his tensed shoulders. "You're killing me here...yes, or...?"

Had he really just refused to acknowledge the possibility she would say "no"?

She reached for the kimono, hoping if it could wrap around his broad shoulders, it would fit her, too. "I don't even know your first name," she said, turning her back to him as she slipped her arms into the robe's sleeves. Like her body cared what his name was. She'd been fantasizing about him from the first day she'd met him. And his good manners and frequent smiles had already challenged her resolve more than once to remain as distant from him as she was from her other neighbors.

He hesitated, as if ready to contradict her, but then answered, "Walt."

Oh, God, she *had* blanked on his name!

Not that he seemed to care—she didn't need to see him to know he was smiling—pleasure filled his voice, the tenor and warmth enough to leave her sleepy and weak. But how could she acquiesce after all this time trying to be invisible to him?

Trying but not wanting. She squelched the traitorous thought with a flick of her shoulders.

"It says 'G. Diaz' on your mailbox." She turned around to find his hand extended to help her up, the line of his arm a direct draw to the thick bottom swell of his erection and the heavy handful of balls. Praying he hadn't caught the direction of her gaze, Bryce offered a nervous smile and shook her head "no". Diaz's hauling her up from the patio was not an option.

"I prefer 'Walt'," he answered and folded his hands behind his back, the motion pushing his cock closer.

"Well, someone has to." A tiny snort possessed her at the thought of someone so sexy being named "Walt". Of all the little bedroom—shower, living room and kitchen— fantasy names she'd dreamt up for G. Diaz, "Walt" wasn't anywhere close to being on the list. Hell, even "Geronimo" had suggested itself.

"It's the Anglicization of 'Galtero'," he explained.

"Why'd you choose that?"

"You know you're just stalling, Bryce." He tilted his head and winked at her before his gaze dropped to where her hands clutched the edges of the kimono together. He hadn't been gentleman enough to find the sash for her, she noted.

"Uhm...no. I wouldn't call it stalling. You want me to strip for you," she answered. "Well...strip again. And yet I don't really know anything about you."

"Not from a lack of trying on my part." Leaning back against the apartment's exterior wall, he folded his arms over his chest. "And, to answer your question, do I look like a 'Galtero Diaz'?"

He looked, she thought, like a wonderful mix of many things. She knew he was paler in winter—at least he had been when he moved in. But right now the olive green eyes were set deep in a face tanned to a burnished gold-brown she couldn't hope to achieve with her wholly Germanic heritage. His hair was a pure jet black that, when he tilted his head like he just had, threw off natural highlights of deep silver. And he was certainly taller than any of the Hispanic men she knew. He must be pushing 6'3".

She shrugged. "Maybe a little, Walt."

"So now that you know my first name, what else is it going to take to get you naked and inside my apartment?"

He threw another bad boy wink at her and Bryce realized she was enjoying the way Walt was playing with her. She looked down to where her bare foot brushed against the linen. That couldn't really be the key, could it?

What else could it be?

Bryce gave a weak nod in the direction of the fabric and bracelet. "I guess you could start by getting a bag for those?"

"Is that a 'yes'?"

The grin he offered was infectious and she forced herself not to return his smile. "It's a 'maybe'," she answered.

He was still smiling, seemed incapable of doing anything else. "Better than a 'no'."

Holding one hand up, he cautioned her against running away. When she promised she wouldn't, he dashed back into the apartment. Returning a few seconds later, he scooped the fabric and bracelet into the bag and offered it to her.

"Could you carry it inside, too?" She felt slightly paranoid, but even the brief contact of the material against her foot had threatened another psychedelic panorama.

Walt bowed and extended his arm toward the apartment's interior in invitation. She wanted to reach out and put the palm of her hand flat against the tanned muscles of his back, feel them ripple as he straightened. She wanted to run her finger down his body, just as he had stroked her. And then she wanted him naked and flat on his back, her tongue teasing the full circumference of his balls before she licked her way up to his swollen cockhead.

"Still not sure?" he asked.

His low purr brushed against her visions of him staked out on the patio's rough concrete. Blushing, she dipped her head and stepped inside the apartment. She was going to embarrass herself—badly—if she didn't stop fantasizing about him immediately.

Stopping in front of the black leather couch, she turned and frowned at him. With the patio door open the last fifteen or so minutes, the apartment's interior had lost its air conditioned coolness. She grimaced at the thought of her bare flesh against the leather, of the way it would stick and peel in a drawn out manner when she moved, reminding him of how much flesh she had just hidden inside his kimono. "Where do you want me?"

"In my bed."

Dizzy, instantly so, she leaned against the couch. "Excuse me?"

"Oh...it's...uhm." He stopped and a golden peach blushed beneath his tan. He pointed in the direction of a closed door. "It's the richest looking room in the apartment, which goes with the style I had in mind."

Brows raised, she scanned the front room and kitchen. The furnishings were far removed from what she would consider inexpensive. The leather couch was part of a three piece set accompanied by a solid mahogany coffee and end tables. A mahogany entertainment center housed a sound system and twenty-one inch television. She hadn't been in that many of the neighboring apartments, but she was pretty sure their interior furnishings were more like her own—a mismatch of self-assembly pressboard papered with wood grain. Next to the closed bedroom door was another room that seemed to serve as a makeshift studio with a second easel and some blank canvases in view. So, he essentially had two bedrooms, while the cost of just a one-bedroom apartment made Bryce forego a car.

"I never see you go to anything that looks like a job," she said, disbelieving he paid for everything just from commissioned portraits. He did go out for extended periods, often returning late at night, but the hours seemed too erratic for work or partying.

"Oh, I paint here or at the client's place, depends on where and when the muse claims me." He had moved to the master bedroom's door, one hand holding the small bag with the sheet and chain, the other resting on the doorknob. "You don't mean to tell me that you've been paying attention?"

Her turn to blush—again. She looked away and hoped he hadn't caught her body's involuntary confession of just how much attention she'd been paying to his schedule.

"I'm just naturally observant," she said when she could tell he wouldn't move until she answered.

"'Naturally observant'...really? So all the times I've tried to get you to talk to me over the last seven months for more than a minute at a time—you were flat out avoiding me?"

He opened the door and the click of the handle drew her attention back to where he stood. Her gaze landed on the sculpted lines of his bronze-colored shoulder. His body partially blocked her view of the bedroom beyond, but, from what she could see, they went together—Diaz and the room. The four-poster bed and dresser had been shaped from dark mahogany that matched the living room set. The bed coverings were a cascade of burgundies and chocolates in silk and velvet, with a touch of dark purple and gold trim. The room and its owner were both rich in texture and color, their surfaces demanding to be touched and admired.

"Well, if you won't answer, will you at least come and lie down?" He moved to the bed and began to mess it up, pushing one side of the bedspread and top sheet toward the center until he had shaped a den for her to nestle in.

"I won't answer because you're fibbing." Surely all those "hellos" of his when they passed going to or from their apartments had merely been good manners on his part? And she'd mainly given him mumbled replies in return, hoping it would sink in that she didn't need him to waste his time on her even if his little attentions fueled her hopeful fantasies.

"No, Bryce, I'm not." He was staring at her again, eyes roaming her body. Her face, the bit of exposed cleavage where she held the robe shut, her hips and the bare curving legs. He gave the bag a little shake. "Where do you want the toga and bracelet?"

Shit, he was holding proof that she hadn't hallucinated Percy's visit. And if the muse's accoutrements were the cause of his intense interest, how long would the effect last if she wasn't wearing them? When would he notice the too small breasts mismatched with wide hips and a stomach that curved out as much as her ass did?

"Earth to Bryce." He spoke softly, his attention still occupied with absorbing the details of her body.

She stared at him, her mind blank with rising panic. "What?" she managed after a few more seconds of silence.

"The toga, where do you want it?"

"Is that what it's called?" she asked, stalling while she looked for someplace to put it where she could touch it without him noticing.

Surprising her, he blushed as he answered. "Technically, no. Women...well, most women, didn't wear togas."

The way he lowered his gaze disarmed her and she took a wild guess at the cause of his sudden embarrassment. "You mean only disreputable women wore togas?"

Diaz took a deep breath and looked back up. She felt the heat of that slowly raised gaze and the strength of her body's reaction.

"Or the occasional goddess." He didn't give her time to fumble out a response. He blinked, then grinned at her. "So where do you want it?"

"The bag?" she asked. Just to be sure. If he was offering something else...

He nodded, his smile firmly cemented on his face.

"Under the pillows," she answered, hesitating, knowing it wasn't too late to leave. *If she wanted to.* "I think."

"Sounds like a safe place." He stuck the bag under one of the pillows and then fluffed the rest of them up before patting the mattress.

Slowly, Bryce crossed the room and sat down on the edge of the bed. It was the closest she'd been to him since leaving the patio and every cell of her body was aware that if she moved another inch to the left, she would be touching him. Reaching out, Diaz caressed her white-knuckled hand. She had a death grip on the robe's edges and he whisper stroked the back of her fingers.

"The robe has to come off, Bryce. That's the way it works."

She studied his face. His gaze had taken on a faraway cast. The mouth was soft, contemplative, and she wondered what it would be like to kiss him or have him take the tip of her breast into his mouth. With her body still covered in a light sheen of sweat, she could almost imagine the glide of his tongue over her nipple and up the slope of her breast, climbing until he reached the hollow of her throat. She heaved a big sigh at the thought, her hands beginning to shake.

As her grip on the robe's edges loosened, Diaz slipped two fingers into one of her palms and gently tugged. Slowly she let him lead her hand down to the mattress. He dropped to his knees and wrapped one hand around the wrist that still clutched the robe closed at her waist while his other hand pushed back the fabric to expose her left breast.

He pulled his bottom lip into his mouth, the way he had on the patio, and Bryce felt fresh cream slickening the inside folds of her labia. He certainly didn't look *painterly* right now. Not with the way he stared at her erect nipple, his grip on her wrist tightening while he sucked and chewed at his bottom lip.

"You're trembling."

"I'm nervous." *And wet and wondering if there are any perks to the job Percy neglected to mention.* But, then, Percy had pretty much neglected to mention anything and everything.

He stopped working his bottom lip and the grin returned in a flash. This time, the way he smiled at her was downright wicked. "We could both be naked if it would help?"

She shook her head "no", vigorously. Her pussy already contracted wildly this close to him, if she saw him naked and erect, she would either come or faint on the spot. Her free hand moved to cover her exposed breast and Diaz stepped back, hands raised in surrender. He walked to the dresser, took a bronzed silk shawl folded over the edge of the mirror and brought it back to the bed. He draped the shawl across her lap and then turned his back to her.

"We'll go in steps then," he suggested. "Why don't you take the robe off, lie down and cover what you want with the silk?"

Holding the shawl against her torso, she loosely folded the robe up and put it at the end of the bed. She caught his gaze in the mirror, dark and smoky as he cheated and watched her.

"Close your eyes," she said and waited until he complied before stretching out in the nest of blankets and drawing the shawl across her mound and breasts. "I'm sorry, I don't mean to be so difficult."

"It's okay. I knew you'd be a challenge."

"I see." *So, Sir Diaz, why did you climb Mount Bryce? Because she was big and she was there!*

Diaz turned and looked at her, his sensuous mouth turned down at the corners. "What do you mean, 'I see'?"

Bryce shrugged, careful not to unsettle the slip of silk protecting her from another round of complete exposure. The bed was long and wide and her backside curved against the small wall of bedcovers. That left a gap at the edge of the bed and Diaz sat down, slowly reaching for one corner of the shawl.

"You said I could cover what I want," she reminded him.

The frown righted itself, his olive green gaze sparkling with quiet intent. "Yes-s-s-s," he said, and grinned wider with each second he elongated the word. "That was step one. Step two, I get to uncover some of what I want."

Diaz moved slowly, giving Bryce time to object or accustom herself to the increased nudity. His eyes followed his hand, first his fingertips grazing her breast and nipple, then his gaze stopping to stroke the surface of her bared skin.

"Your coloring is lovely, Bryce." He reached up to curve a lock of her hair along the side of her cheek. "All honeyed-blonde up top." He trailed his fingertip down the sensitive skin of her throat, back to the tip of her peaked nipple. She gasped but he didn't pull away. "And cream and cherries everywhere else."

If he only knew how cherry, she thought, straining against the impulse to arch her back and press her breast against his open palm. Could he smell how wet she was? Her body was warm and melting despite the coolness of the apartment now that the air conditioner had kicked back on.

He drew the shawl down over the swell of her stomach. Bryce tensed. Afraid that whatever illusion gripped him would shatter on so close an inspection, her hand crept under the pillow to find the toga and bracelet.

"Yes, I like that." He caught her hand. "But above the pillow and a little over your head."

Leaning forward, he steadied himself with one hand against her hip. His fingers lightly pressed into her skin in a possessive curl while he positioned her arm to curve around her face until he had her hand tangled in the soft waves of her hair. The movement brought his chest into contact with hers and she closed her eyes. His hand on her hip, his arm enclosing hers, body to body, it felt like a lovers' embrace. She breathed in the scent of him, becoming increasingly detached from everything else in the room. In the air surrounding him, she could smell a trace of the paints he worked with on the patio. But closer to his skin, she detected the warm perfume of toasted almonds, and his hair held the rose-watermelon smell of guava.

Taking her other arm, he positioned it along the curve of her waist and hip, her hand resting over the warm section of flesh he had just held. She pressed the loose smile forming at the corners of her mouth into an ambivalent line before he could see the effect he had on her.

She noticed the stiff way he rose from the mattress and walked to the corner chair and believed for the moment that his wasn't the only magic being worked in the room. Gripping the chair, he started dragging it closer to the bed. The muscles of his back bulged, narrowing his waist until her gaze was forced down to where the cotton shorts clung to his butt and upper thighs.

The cushioned chair's width was somewhere in between a regular chair and a loveseat, and he used his whole body to move it. Dressed, she would have offered to help him. Naked on his bed and with his back turned to her, she relished every flex and muscle bulge the effort produced.

When the chair was angled about a foot from the bed's end, he went back to the corner and retrieved a standing lamp. Repositioning the light closer to Bryce, he tilted the shade until her body was lit in a soft glow. She expected him, at this point, to leave the room for supplies, but he reached under the bed and pulled out a sketch pad and box of charcoals, instead.

"Don't you need your easel?" she asked. "And paints?"

Diaz sank into the plush padding of the chair. He pushed a chin-length lock of hair, black as a raven's wing, behind his ear and rested one foot against the bed's bottom frame. Radiating a proprietary ease over the entire room, he flipped open the sketch book and thumbed past already filled pages. "Some preliminary drawings," he answered, finding a clean sheet. "Easier to undo my mistakes when they're in charcoal and not oil."

Concerned that she'd started a process that would last beyond the weekend, Bryce started to turn onto her side, but his upward glance froze her in place. "Well, how long does all this take?" she asked as she settled back into the pose.

She couldn't describe the expression Diaz wore while she waited for him to answer. He looked like he was holding a fresh chilled strawberry in his mouth, the juices spreading across his tongue while the pressure of his sensuously curving smile slowly crushed the fruit between tongue and upper palate. Sated, happy and more than just a little horny—that's how he looked.

"Oh, a finished painting takes months," he answered at last.

Months! She certainly didn't have that long. Percy's impromptu vacation didn't give her more than a few days. "I'm not sure I have more than the weekend."

"If the weekend is all you're willing to allow me, I'll take it." He dropped his gaze to the sketch pad and began making the first strokes. "For now."

Chapter Three

Trying to sketch and hide his growing erection with the art pad at the same time, Walt shifted in his seat. Every stroke of the charcoal across the page equaled pressure instantly transferred to the bottom edge of the pad where it rubbed against his cock. He'd painted plenty of nudes, even women he had been intimate with. He had always been able to view them with a sense of artistic abstraction during the sessions. But he had never painted a woman he had been lusting after for months. To go from a complete standstill to this...

And Bryce wasn't making it any easier on him. She was thinking things, he could tell. The color on her breasts and face would rise from its usual warm cream to a rosy pink. Naughty things? Shy things? That he didn't know, but his cock grew incrementally harder with each blush. Lines blurred on the page and a slight tremor ran through his hand. He wasn't sure whether he could actually sketch her when she was within touching distance.

Maybe if he hadn't already touched her, he could have remained detached. But it was too late for "maybes", and he would be lying to himself if he didn't admit to wanting her first as a lover. He could still smell the gentle fragrances of her body from when he had briefly pressed against her. Far from the juicy cherry coloring of her lips and nipples, she carried the scent of wild jasmine resting on top of cut green apples. The difference created a startling impression of innocence that was completely at odds with the suggestively lush flesh and the things he imagined doing with her.

Looking at her on the bed, he saw that she was lost in thought again and he waited for her to come out of it, waited to catch the slow spread of color against the creamy skin and see the barely perceptible swell of the breasts that bordered on petite in their asymmetry to the rest of her body. He groaned in anticipation, the sound seeming to jerk her back to reality. *There. The flush.* His cock twitched and he groaned again before dragging his attention back down to the sketch pad.

"Is something wrong?"

Concern darkened her hazel irises and he gave his head a slow shake to let her know everything was okay. *It was damn near perfect.*

"You're sure?"

Well, he wanted her to lose the damn shawl, but then he might come completely undone—scaring her and embarrassing himself in the process. And she would bolt if he came on too strong. He didn't doubt that for a second. She would be up and out, and he'd be right back at square one, facing untold months of offering to drive her someplace or help her carry something in or out of her apartment. The guarded smiles she had always returned would change, too, growing more distant or, perhaps, downright hostile.

"Yeah, I'm sure." His chest tightened at the need to tell her otherwise. He tried to keep his mouth shut, but his tongue escaped for an instant to wet the center of his pressed lips. The act seemed to trigger a full body blush in her, the rush of color followed a second later by the smell of her arousal.

He'd have to be stupid not to know she was aroused, and that she would never admit to it on her own. Yet, no matter how much she sat there in innocent denial, her body scented the air with the smell of her readiness. He wanted to test the air, see if it was ripe with more than just the smell of her pussy. He imagined sticking his tongue out and being able to taste her cream.

His balls contracted at the thought and he dropped the piece of charcoal he was holding into its box. Flipping the sketch pad's cover back, he pressed it against his groin and hoped she hadn't noticed his hard need. He glanced at the clock. This had to be, he mused, the longest straight period of time he'd had an erection since junior high. That had been the day he'd discovered that girls didn't really have cooties.

"How about a break?" he suggested. "We've been going at it for almost two hours."

Bryce nodded. "I am getting a little stiff."

Stiff, hah! Her choice of words only increased his awareness of how hard he'd become looking at her. He could teach her a thing or two about *stiff* right now, he thought before realizing she was watching him. He dipped his head to avoid meeting her gaze; it wouldn't do to have both of them blushing like teenagers.

"Hungry or thirsty?" he asked and smoothed the cover to the sketch pad. "I'm a pretty good cook."

"I ate just before invading your patio."

It took her a little too long to answer and he wondered if she was telling the truth. "I can't tempt you with one of my specialties?"

"Uhm...no. I think I'd like to grab a set of clothes and check my email."

She pulled the shawl up. The firm breasts and peaked nipples disappeared beneath the fabric. Another quaint blush colored her cheeks and her hand discreetly skipped down to make sure she hadn't pulled the shawl up too high.

"I teach G.E.D. prep classes," she explained. "And my students start peppering me with questions Friday night." Sitting up, she grabbed the kimono and held it to her, her expectant gaze asking him to leave the room.

"You could check it from my computer," Walt offered. "And I can go back through the patio to get your clothes— don't want you getting scratched up any more than you already are."

"No. That won't—that's okay," she answered. "I think my front door is unlocked anyway."

She had winced in answering him, and Walt's mind immediately conjured up images of nylons and lingerie drying on makeshift lines inside the apartment. Or maybe, he thought, she didn't want him opening her dresser. Maybe she kept *toys* inside her dresser. After all, he'd never seen a man entering or leaving her apartment, and a woman her age certainly had to have needs.

He cleared his throat, tried to mentally dislodge the picture of her pleasuring herself. He needed to stay focused on keeping her in his apartment. She wasn't being the wary, sensible Bryce who had treated him to little more than short, shy smiles and the occasional lingering gaze for the last seven months. He didn't want her coming back to her senses any time soon, and that was almost certain to happen once she was back in her apartment.

But she seemed determined to get out. She glanced around the room and pointed at his clock. It was just shy of eight. "How about I come back at eight forty-five?" she asked. "That'll give me time to shower and get the dirt out of the scratches."

Walt relented. He didn't want to push too hard, and, by setting a time, she'd given him a ready-made excuse to knock on her door if she stayed away longer than she'd agreed. Lord knew he could certainly use a shower himself. There was no way he was going to make it through another round of sketching her if he didn't relieve a little tension first. He held out a few more seconds before relenting.

"But you *will* come back, right?" Christ, had he really asked her like that? So much for trying to play it cool. But he'd wasted more than half a year trying to play it cool with her, waiting for her to melt as most women did. She'd be back in her safe little apartment already if he hadn't been so forward on the patio, touching her and telling her directly that he wanted to paint her nude.

Bryce nodded and he knew instantly the old Bryce was resurfacing—her consent so slow and shy that he was rock hard again. He jumped from the chair, sketch pad tight against his crotch as he fumbled out the words that he would leave her alone to dress. He caught the door on his way out, closing it behind him and immediately collapsing against the frame for support. He tossed the pad halfway across the room to the leather recliner and then pulled back the waist band to his cotton shorts. He wasn't small by any means, but he'd never seen his cock this swollen with need, the length further elongated and curving back to touch his navel in its search for a warm, moist pocket in which to bury itself.

Slowly he replaced the elastic waist band against his skin and then ran a shaking hand along his jaw line. If she was going to keep having this effect on him, Walt thought, he needed a bigger sketch pad.

▦ ▦ ▦

As soon as the door closed, Bryce whipped the robe around her body. She needed to pee badly, or at least felt like it. Her body had rollercoastered through so many highs and lows of sexual tension since she'd landed on Diaz's patio that she wasn't quite sure what her clit was feeling now. She just knew there was pressure to relieve. A lot of pressure.

Covered by the robe, she quickly scanned the room for something to serve as a makeshift sash. She saw the robe's regular sash, instead, rolled tight and resting on the nightstand next to the bed. She spent another minute threading the sash and tieing a tight bow, and then she plucked the plastic bag from beneath the pillow case. She'd lock herself in the bathroom at home and try either the toga or the chain on. Percy had said a muse must wear the whole uniform. Bryce might be crazy enough—or desperate enough from her infatuation with Diaz—to accept the proposition that Percy was more than a nut job. That didn't, however, mean Bryce was ready to risk her sanity wholesale by putting the toga and bracelet on at the same time. And Diaz seemed able to work just by Bryce having the items near her—for the most part. He did pause a lot.

Stop thinking and get moving!

Holding the bag away from her, she crossed to the bedroom door. Diaz was on the couch, his head in one hand, his other hand holding a pillow over his lap.

Probably cursing himself and wondering just what the hell he agreed to, she thought. She forced a smile and bobbed her head in the direction of the bedroom. "Eight forty-five, right?"

Hearing his mumbled agreement, she retreated out the front door.

Chapter Four

The door to Bryce's apartment was unlocked and she entered holding the bag in front of her at full arm's length. She ignored the fierce need to pee that pinched at her sides and clit, and decided to lock the front and patio doors before securing herself in the bathroom. Only then would it be relatively safe to try on either the toga or bracelet.

At least, that was her plan.

"What in the name of *Hades* are you doing holding sacred artifacts like they were a bag of dog shit!"

The voice, deep throated but matronly, roared the question and Bryce spun around to find herself facing a very angry Greek. At least the woman looked Greek. Her toga was a pale semi-transparent rose, and a wreath of the same flower crowned her head. One firm breast was exposed, the other guarded by a strip of fabric and the lyre she held close to her body. Far from Percy's waif-like form, the woman was full-bodied. Almost six feet tall, her limbs were all soft curves. The outline of thighs visible through the fabric reminded Bryce of the down pillows she had splurged on for her bedroom a few months ago. If Percy truly was the real deal, Bryce had a feeling the woman standing before her was a little higher up in the Muse hierarchy.

The woman's stance softened and she took the bag from Bryce. "One of the originals, in fact," she said and removed the ruined toga.

Damn, this mind reading thing is starting to piss me off, Bryce thought and then took a startled breath as she realized she might as well have said it out loud.

The woman chuckled, the sound an erotic purr that had Bryce backing toward the apartment door.

"Not so fast, youngling." She held out her hand, her air imperious until Bryce relented and accepted it. "My name is Erato. Normally one of Percy's little indiscretions would be Thalia's business, but, today, you get me."

"S-so you'll take the toga and chain back and this will all be over, right?" Bryce asked. A sudden hollowing in the pit of her stomach made her wonder whether "over" was what she wanted.

"Again, youngling, you move too fast." Still holding the toga and the bag with the bracelet inside, Erato walked over to Bryce's laptop and jiggled the mouse. The blank screen Bryce had been staring at when Percy first knocked flickered into view.

"You're taking this awfully well," Erato offered, looking from the screen to Bryce. "Even those expecting the robe have a hard time adjusting to the real existence of muses."

Bryce shrugged. "Except for when I was wearing that stuff, I felt like I was in control—so it didn't matter if it was real or not." Her hand danced, grasping for a better answer. "I mean, if I'm having a nervous breakdown or something—it's not all that bad."

Erato turned and looked at the wall Bryce shared with Diaz, her expression fixed as if she were looking through the wall. "Not bad, indeed."

The purr was back in the muse's voice and doing weird things to Bryce's ability to concentrate. She didn't think it was relevant that she was heterosexual, the woman gave off an understated sexuality that wormed its way into Bryce's body. And Erato knew it, the sense of command clearly written across her face as she turned back to Bryce.

"If I let you off the hook, I'm failing your new friend in there," Erato started, "failing you, too, I think."

Bryce shook her head. "I'm not an artist or anything like that...I just teach."

For a second, Bryce thought she saw understanding in Erato's expression, but then the muse tilted her chin up and the feeling disappeared. Erato ran a finger across the blank Word file displaying on the screen.

"How long have you had this writing assignment?"

"Six weeks," Bryce answered. If she didn't have a completed short story to turn in Monday, she'd fail the class and have to enroll in the fall semester to finish her master's degree. She was already a couple years older than everyone in her class, another five months to finish seemed like an eternity of waiting.

"And you've been trying all that time?"

Desperately.

"Six weeks and not one word." Erato ran her finger across the screen again, the display filling with one of Bryce's critical essays on the hidden structure in and between Kafka's short stories. "And yet you know how to write...very well in fact."

"Different." *Is this how muses work? Through nagging?*

A sharp smile crinkled the skin around her eyes as Erato waggled a finger at Bryce. "If I choose to 'work' on you, you'll know it," she warned. "Your ass will be sore from twelve hours in this chair. When you stand up, your body will be bent at the waist and unable to straighten. You'll take a notepad into the toilet with you or carry the laptop in."

"You'll walk through the grocery store babbling, laughing and crying right along with your characters." Letting the screen go blank again, she advanced on Bryce. "You won't be able to see anything without it reminding you of something else, until you're tied up in a daisy chain of ideas and connections and 'what ifs'."

Chastised, Bryce dropped her gaze. "So, what is it you want, then?" She had no doubt Erato wanted something specific from her. It seemed to be the weekend's theme.

"I want you," Erato began, her tone sweet and forgiving, "to continue playing Diaz's muse. All weekend. If he wants you completely stripped, you'll do it. No more hiding beneath the shawl. If he wants you standing on tiptoe holding a bowl of fruit for five hours, you'll do it."

Bryce gave an unsure nod.

"And, in exchange, you'll have a passing story turned in on time Monday afternoon."

"That seems a little...uneven."

Digging the chain from the bottom of the plastic bag, Erato smiled. "True, but I don't think I have enough time to wring a better deal from you." Bracelet in hand, she pointed at Bryce's bathroom door. "Now, go clean up while I fix these things."

Erato's presence reinforced the fact that the toga and bracelet had real power, and Bryce froze at the thought of having to put either back on. "I don't think I can," she whispered, her voice descending to the pitch of a frightened two-year-old.

Erato was pulling the charms from the bracelet one by one and shrugged off Bryce's concern with a quick roll of her shoulders. "I'll take care of their effect on you," she promised. "Now go—and for Aphrodite's sake, don't put those damn jeans and sweatshirt back on."

▨ ▨ ▨

Bryce emerged from the shower to find a champagne-colored cinch blouse and a flared skirt of the same color on a hanger hooked to the back of the bathroom door. Neither had come from her closet—both were completely unlike anything she owned or would consider buying. Nor was there a panty or bra in sight. Wrapping a towel around her body, Bryce found Erato waiting on the other side of the bathroom door. The muse pushed into the room and grabbed the hanger.

"You don't need panties or a bra," Erato said, anticipating her complaint. "You're going to be stripping, remember? And you don't need the support up top."

"It just seems a little gauche," Bryce said. It was true, though. For all her size, she was smaller up top, her body widening around her waist to begin the bottom drop of a pear.

"Bryce, hon, you have to start working what you were born with—not wrapping it up in bulky clothes." Erato held her hands up, gave her hips a little shake and then smiled. "Now, doesn't that look better?"

Bryce looked down to find herself dressed in the blouse and skirt. She looked up, the mist sufficiently cleared from the mirror for her to see that the diagonal slash of the cinch blouse cut across her cleavage and down to her left side. The top exposed a soft-V of flesh, making her shoulders look narrower and presenting the top swell of her breasts.

"You've got great tits, hon," Erato said and cupped Bryce's left breast. "I should know, I've helped write a couple hundred odes to breasts. Small ones, big ones, pale and dark." She finished with a little squeeze that made Bryce feel like she was at an awards show. "Each set is its own work of art and these are beyond nice."

"Flawless skin, too," she added. "And hazel eyes! They call those bedroom eyes, did you know that?" Erato thrust her head closer to Bryce and threw her hands up in despair. "You don't get it, do you? Beauty isn't just one thing and it isn't the same for everyone...like that nasty little Kipling wrote...'a fool there was and he made his prayer to a rag and a bone and a hank of hair; we called her the woman who did not care, but the fool he called her his lady fair'."

Feeling like she'd just swallowed a mouthful of milk past its expiration date, Bryce took a step away from Erato. "I get that you're comparing me to a rag and a bone—"

"By Zeus, you're dense!"

"And you can stop with the name dropping, okay?" Bryce said. "I don't know enough about all of you to be impressed any more than I already am. Just tell me that you've fixed the damn toga and Diaz can get his painting while I get my passing grade."

"Well, fine." Erato sniffed, the sound an indignant little puff. "If you're only in it for the grade. Not like you've apparently learned anything at college, anyway."

From her robes, she pulled out a bracelet and shoved it at Bryce. "Here, I've pared the original down *a bit.*"

Bryce looked at the bracelet while Erato unhooked a charm from her own bracelet. The silver and gold formed two-thirds of a simple braid. The third strand was made up of linen thread suspiciously like that of the toga. The string of linen was itself a braid, making a total of three strands times three.

"There were nine of us, you know, in the beginning," Erato said as she took the bracelet back and attached her charm to it. "The arts were simple back then. It was easy and we became victims of our own success, inspiring new art forms. We had to branch out, taking on assistants who could specialize. Percy is one of Thalia's protégés, though she wants to be one of mine. All told, the original nine supervise close to seven hundred assistants."

"What do you do?" Bryce asked, trying to make small talk as she nervously watched Erato secure the charm bracelet to her wrist. When Erato was done, Bryce examined the solitary charm—a dove done in mother of pearl. No sights or sounds took possession of her and she relaxed.

"Why don't you buy a book and find out, Ms. Grad Student?" Erato turned with a little "hmmph", apparently ready to pop out as quickly as she had popped in. Stopping, she eyed Bryce over her shoulder. "Don't forget—if he wants you on tiptoe with a bowl of fruit?"

"I'll do it," Bryce answered.

"And your assets?"

"I'll...uhm...work them." Bryce paused and gave the charm bracelet a little shake. "But, is that really necessary with this?" The glare Erato shot her made Bryce tuck her hand behind her back. *Guess so.*

"Oh, and one last thing, hon?"

The woman's grin was downright lecherous and Bryce hesitated to answer. "Yes?"

"Don't overthink the size of his sketchpad."

🁢 🁢 🁢

Bryce stood for a few stunned seconds watching the empty space where Erato had been. Sure that her big, bad muse had actually left, she ducked into her bedroom for a pair of sandals.

And some panties, she silently amended.

She pulled open the closet door and bent to rummage through the pile of shoes that constantly littered the floor. Except, the pile of shoes was gone and a single pair of gold strapped sandals stood spotlighted from the closet's bare light bulb. She picked the shoes up and examined them. A soft suede lined the inside of the straps and the soles were thickly cushioned to absorb her weight without pinching her spine. The gold-tone surface was subdued, beautiful in a discreet way.

"Easy choice." Trying to suppress a grin, she dropped the sandals onto the floor and slipped them on before walking to her dresser. Opening the top drawer, the grin fell from her face.

"She stole my panties?" Bryce looked up at the ceiling, shaking her fist, a string of sailor-sanctioned words lining up along her tongue.

The alarm clock blared. She hadn't set an alarm and the sound jarred all the righteous fury from her. Bryce bounced across the bed, slapped the switch off and swore when she saw what time it was. It was eight fifty—making her five minutes late already. Turning on the bed, she slid back across it, dashed through the living room and grabbed her house keys from the hook by the door.

Outside, she locked the first deadbolt and stepped three feet to the right and knocked on Diaz's door.

Chapter Five

"You came back?"

"I'm here, aren't I?" Feeling like the magic of Erato's visit still cloistered her, Bryce turned the answer into a tease. Her body brushed his, slow and lingering, as she entered the apartment and placed her keys on the hook next to his. Damned if he hadn't looked relieved to see her. When he didn't say anything, she turned to find him staring at her.

"That dress..." he started. His gaze widened and slowly moved down her body. He stopped at the show of cleavage where the blouse's front panel crossed over her breast and wrapped around her waist. His mouth pushed forward, the pucker wistful as he studied the rounded flare of her hips and thighs. He smiled at the gold sandals and then moved back up her body in the same deliberate crawl. "It's really...*wow*," he finished.

Feeling a slow blush heat her cheeks, she gave a soft "thank you", and moved into the living room.

"It's new?" he asked. His voice sounded relatively sure it was new. When Bryce nodded "yes", confirming his suspicion, a frown pulled at the corners of his full mouth. "Who's it for?"

Impatient for him to leave the security of the door, she moved closer to the bedroom. "Tonight, it's for you, at least for the next few minutes."

His expression slid to confused, and Bryce sighed. "You do still want me in your bed?" Her wrist itched where the bracelet touched it and she gave an irritated twitch of her hand. Had she really just asked him if he wanted her in his bed?

Must be the bracelet talking. It sure didn't sound like something she'd say.

"Right, yes!" Diaz answered, locking the door and closing in on her at last.

She could almost hear the exclamation point at the end of his sentence, and the wolfish gleam in his eyes had her gripping the doorframe. The thought that she was making him hot, even with the bracelet's help, had cream sliding past the seal of her labia to wet her thighs. "Sorry I was a little late," she murmured as he opened the bedroom door for her.

Diaz put his hand against the small of her back, guiding her into the room and toward the bed. She could feel the heat in his touch and the muscles in her legs turned to warmed jelly.

"Worth the wait, I assure you," he said.

It might have sounded like a stock phrase some smooth-talker would offer, but it was coming from Diaz. He was smooth without being a smooth-talker. She sat down and watched him move about the room as he changed the position of the lights to account for the growing outside shadows that had found their way inside.

While he was pre-occupied with the lighting, she studied him. He was still shirtless but had switched into long black pants after his shower. The pants were satiny and loose, but the way they sought after his skin easily suggested the silhouette of his powerful thighs and calves. His hair hadn't dried and naturally gathered at the back of his neck, dipping between his shoulder blades in a small "v". Sparkling beads of moisture dotted his back, shoulders and chest like freckles, filling Bryce with the urge to lick them away.

When he pulled a new sketch pad from beneath the bed and placed it on the chair, she had to choke back her surprise. She would have guessed the first pad to measure around eleven by fourteen inches. The new pad must have been at least eighteen by twenty four. The switch was definitely something she would have noticed and spent hours overthinking if Erato hadn't warned her in advance. Even with the warning, curiosity pricked at her. But then he turned back to readjust the light— presenting the profile of his body to her—and she understood the reason for the bigger pad. He didn't need wider paper to sketch her body; the boy had a steel beam down his pants he was trying to hide.

Satisfied at last with the lighting, he faced her and she slammed shut her wide-eyed, open-mouthed appreciation before he could catch the direction of her gaze.

"So, you want me to leave for a few seconds?" he asked and gestured at her clothing.

Already? she wondered. But, then, hadn't she rushed him into the bedroom?

Bryce looked around, searching for the shawl despite Erato's admonition. When she didn't see it, she glanced up at him. Guilty and hopeful, his expression told her he'd put the shawl away.

"I thought, if you came back, you wouldn't need it," he said. His eyelids fluttered slowly, like a butterfly in a snow storm, its wings weighted down. "I want to see all of you, Bryce."

She felt as if he'd just body slammed her, the need in his voice soft yet forceful. Each word carried a heavy sensuality. It almost hurt to listen to him and she was sure that denying him would be an exquisite torture.

Well, at least he wasn't holding a fruit bowl out—yet. Even though she had spent less than half an hour in the muse's company, she wouldn't put it past Erato to meddle and pop the idea into his head. Relenting, Bryce nodded at the door as she reached for the edge of her blouse. "It'll just take me a couple seconds. I'll call you when I'm ready."

A visible reluctance weighed his feet down as he left the room—as if he was as eager for the unveiling as he was to have her posed naked on his bed. She hurried him out of the room with an impatient wave. When his compliance ended just across the room's threshold, she made a sweeping motion to have him close the door. The last thing she saw was a bad boy grin surface on his face. The grin made his eyes seem to shine brighter, and a responsive heat flared between her thighs.

Alone and shyly aware of her aroused state, she removed her clothes slower than she intended. She'd be completely exposed again, especially the parts that weren't included in Erato's little list of Bryce's "assets". Once she was completely undressed, but for the bracelet, she carefully folded the clothes and placed them on the open shelf of his nightstand. Reclining against the bedcovers, she tried to place her hand across her mons in a casual position. It rested there with all the grace of a department store mannequin's. Snorting with self-irritation, she tried merely to relax her hand.

She called out to him, too soft and nervous the first time so that she had to repeat herself. "I'm ready."

His return was quick, telling her that he had been waiting just outside the door, as eager to begin, perhaps, as she was to delay. Seeing that she wasn't in the same position, he stopped at the side of the chair. "I want you in the same pose," he said.

Bryce nodded but didn't move—couldn't move. And Diaz was only making it worse with the thoughtful way he sucked at his bottom lip. She could feel him pulling her in with each suck. She watched the bottom lip emerge wet, and the thin layer of gloss mesmerized her.

"Nervous all over again?"

Bryce swallowed. "Yeah. Terrified if you want to know the truth."

Diaz approached the bed and sat down next to her, his hands held tightly in his lap. "Why?"

She arched one brow at him as if the simple expression would convey how rude it was for him to make her confess more. But he seemed to understand.

"Bryce, I only paint what's beautiful." He touched her arm, tried to smooth away the tension. "You're beautiful."

She shook off the possibility. "I—I don't even know how to pose."

"I'll pose you." He tried to lift her arm but she stiffened. Drawing back, he rested his chin in his hand and studied her. "Roll to your other side, okay?"

A relieved flush heated her body as she instantly sought to obey him. She wouldn't, at least, have to see him looking at her. The thought was followed a second later by regret. She wouldn't be able to see him at all.

"I imagine you're a quick study," he said.

Bryce felt his weight leave the bed and then she heard him pull something from beneath the bed. There was the crisp brush of paper against paper and she pulled her arms closer to her chest—suddenly and inexplicably nervous. Was he going to show her poses? Of what? Was there a plus-sized *Playboy* she'd never heard of—or, worse yet, some fetish magazine? Dread coated the inside of her stomach.

"Close your eyes," he ordered as she felt his weight return to the mattress.

Once she had complied, he leaned across her several times. His movements and the accompanying sounds gave her the impression that he had opened several books or heavy-bound magazines on the bunched up bedspread in front of her.

Feeling his bare chest against her back each time he placed something else in front of her, Bryce's alarm notched another level higher. How many porn mags...?

His body stretched out alongside hers. The feel of his chest fully against her back and the press of his clothed erection between the cheeks of her bottom cut through the rest of her question. "You can open your eyes now," he whispered against the sensitive skin of her throat.

She took her time obeying him, both afraid of what she'd find and glorying in the heat of his body and the tantalizing whisper of ultra-fine body hair against her. When he prompted her with an "all the way", she sighed and finally looked down at the books in front of her.

Rubens, Pontormo, Titian. Naked women looked up at her, the expressions varying from contentment to passion to indifference. *Leda and the Swan, Venus, Gaia.* All goddesses or the consorts of gods. All beautiful. All like her in their size. Following the books were vintage comics from the sixties, encased in plastic, but their covers filled with Frazetta's voluptuous kick-ass women.

When she shook her head and began explaining that she understood these things in the abstract, Diaz pressed his lips against her ear.

"Just look," he said. He turned the pages of a Rubens book and then rested his hand across her arm. His thumb caressed the bottom curve of her breast, the pad permanently indented from so many hours holding a brush. "What do you see?"

When she didn't answer, he upped the stakes, his hand sliding down the full arc of her hip. "What about them is beautiful to you?"

Shivering from his touch, Bryce looked at Venus as Paris handed the golden apple to her. Hera stood with her back to the artist while Athena looked on, tight lipped. The women's skin glowed, looking soft and lickable. Their full thighs and sturdy calves were distinctly feminine. The faces of the two goddesses facing her were mature, but the bloom was still on their rounded cheeks.

"Okay, what don't you find beautiful about them?" Diaz asked as she remained silent.

Bryce jerked her head down, burrowing against the pillow. There wasn't anything about them that wasn't beautiful. "It's not the same." His persistence had her near tears. "The artists found them beautiful, painted them beautiful."

She felt the exasperated twitch of his cock against her bottom and he buried his face in the bend of her neck. "Bryce, baby." He sighed her name, his grip on her tightening. "I already told you, I think you're beautiful."

And I can find a hundred guys who don't.

She twisted the bracelet around the circle of her wrist a few times and then chewed on an already tattered nail. "Can I keep the bracelet on?" she asked, not quite relenting.

"Of course."

Diaz went to remove one of the books but she stayed his hand.

"Not yet," she said. "I want to look a little more." She wanted him to stay next to her, too, filling the soft valley of her ass with his cock. He had stayed hard the whole time, the knowledge squeezing a contraction from the eager muscles of her cunt.

"It's all so stylized," she said. Running a finger over the image of a reclining woman, she tapped the clean mons. "It's all so powdered and...shaved?"

His cock twitched again, longer and stronger than when it had first jumped against her skin. Her body, disobedient, twitched back, momentarily gripping his erection.

"Let me shave you." The request was whispered. His hand, still on her hip, dropped down to brush once against the blonde fur of her sex.

"If you want me...it, like that," she stammered, "it will take me about fifteen minutes."

"I want to do it." His touch grew bolder, starting first with a brief caress of her inner thigh. He combed his fingers up through her pubic hair, his nails lightly raking her skin. Then he smoothed the hair back down, his first two fingers slipping between the thick folds of her labia to touch her clit.

Bryce jerked against him, her breathing panicky and erratic. Erato couldn't have meant that she yield to any and all requests?

"I need to learn your contours, Bryce." He stroked deeper, his thumb joining the fray to keep the pressure stacked on her clit. He nuzzled her neck, his cock pulsing between her ass cheeks as the strokes to her pussy grew faster.

Panting, she covered his hand with her own, forcing him to still his touch, but not pushing him away. What hadn't he just discovered about her contours? He had worked the exterior of her cunt until she was hovering on the point of orgasm. That should be enough.

"Step over the edge, Bryce." He breathed the words into her ear. "You won't mind the fall—and I'll be right there with you."

"You, you can shave me," was all she could muster. Hell, if he was disgusted with her come Monday, she could always teach English in Japan.

"You're sure?" Wrapped tightly in his growing passion, the question didn't even sound like real words.

"Yes." Bryce wanted to cry. She didn't want to think about why the tears were there, hovering, she only knew that she was oddly relieved when he got up and left the room.

Chapter Six

The books were still open on the bed and Bryce picked them up, trying to find some calm by stacking them into an even line on the floor before she eased them back under the bed. When it sounded like Diaz had finished gathering everything he would need to shave her, she returned to the bed and partially hid beneath the covers. Did he want to do it on the bed? Somewhere else? It seemed like something terribly messy to do outside the bathroom.

Diaz came into the bedroom carrying a bowl filled with water and two towels wrapped around the razor and shaving cream. He placed these on the floor and then turned off all but the standing lamp. Instead of returning to the shaving supplies or telling her where he wanted her, he laid down next to her. He was on his side, one hand propping his head up. He touched his fingertips to her collarbone then slowly trailed them up to her chin. With just his index finger, he stroked her bottom lip.

His gaze drifted between her mouth and eyes. "This is going to be very intimate." When Bryce could only manage a swallow and a nod, he smiled. "So," he asked, "are you going to let me kiss you?"

He was asking permission to kiss her after he'd had his hand between her legs? And yet, she wasn't a virgin *down there*, at least not technically. She'd taken care of that herself. But her mouth—twenty-nine years old and she'd never kissed a boy. How could she confess that? Tell the truth, lie or just say "no"? *No, you can't kiss me. Take my pussy, take my ass, but please don't kiss me.* She didn't think she could stand kissing him tonight and then going back to being near strangers on Monday.

"You look like I just ran your puppy over, Bryce."

His expression was troubled, more so when she answered him.

"I feel like you kinda did," she whispered.

He pulled his hand back to his own body. "Then why are you here?"

Certainly not because of Erato's bribe. She could still remember the first day she'd seen him. It had been the day he'd moved in and she'd cast him as the star of that night's fantasy. Something about that climax had felt utterly *connected*—as if he'd actually done something to give it to her. From that night on, she'd invited no other man into her fantasies and it wasn't long before she'd developed a full-on crush for Diaz.

She'd noticed the way she was never invisible to him despite her best attempts, but she also had noticed the way nothing was invisible to him. And even though the latter realization made her feel a little less special, it didn't lessen the crush. She went to bed thinking about him, particularly following those days when she could hear him working out next door, or when they had passed in the courtyard and she had imagined that his eyes lingered a little longer and a little more favorably than they should have. She'd stroke herself while thinking about him, inside and out. Her fingers became his, the small box of sex toys in her dresser making poor substitutes for his cock.

"You don't even know why?"

Bryce looked at him. The emotions playing across his face confused her. He looked hurt, and she had been the cause. "I know why...I'm just afraid to say it."

Frown lines ran deep across his forehead and he chewed at his bottom lip. A second later, his expression smoothed with determination. He leaned closer to her and curled his hand around her shoulder. "Bryce, I'm going to kiss you unless you tell me not to."

He waited the time it took her to breathe in once, time enough for her to object if she wanted to before he pressed his mouth against hers. The pressure was light at first and then his hand cupped the side of her face. The demand of the kiss intensified, his thumb playing at the corner of her mouth to coax her lips open. She felt his other hand touch the top of her head, the long fingers weaving their way into her hair. His tongue traced the line of her sealed lips, his mouth opening wider to cover hers.

Bryce relaxed and let his tongue sweep gently into her mouth to thrust and lick. She brought her palm against his chest and brushed her fingertips against his hard nipple. Diaz groaned. The vibration filled her mouth and echoed down her throat until she was groaning with him, kissing and thrusting with a matching passion. She dared to touch him lower, her hand traveling down his body to brace against the tightly drawn waist muscles.

Diaz wound his fingers more securely in her hair while his other hand claimed one firm breast. He squeezed, gently, and brought his index and thumb to press against her nipple. It was glorious and disturbing at the same time. Her nipple instantly hardened and she felt as if a live wire had just touched her, its electricity lashing around her body until she shook with its energy. She turned into his touch, a frustrated moan escaping her when her skin came into contact with the satin fabric of his pants. She wanted him equally exposed, wanted to feel the smooth velvet skin of his cock and have it serve as a lightning rod for the uncontrollable power running through her.

He broke the kiss and buried his face in the silky flow of her hair against the pillow. He was panting, still holding her tight, his whole body tense. He slid alongside her until his mouth was against her ear.

"I'm going to come just touching you like this."

Bryce hadn't stopped shaking, the contractions of her pussy hitting hard and vehemently. She squeezed her ass and thighs, trying to master her body's responses, but the pressure and the slide of her labia against her clit threatened to send her spiraling further out of control. She grabbed his ass, her fingertips digging into the firm glutes. The difference in their heights had the jut of his covered erection wedged against the top split of her cunt.

"Don't move," she begged. Another second and she would either be back in control—or coming against him.

※ ※ ※

Walt felt her shudder against him, heard the tremor of air around her mouth as she sucked it in. He remained motionless, his balls drawn tight, and he bit down hard on his top lip to stop the climax that would come with just one more sensual roll of her mound against the head of his cock. His ass tensed and Bryce dug her fingertips in harder, the breath she had been holding leaving her body in one long moan.

God, he wanted to pull his pants down and spread her legs, spearing his cock into the sweet pussy his fingertips had touched less than half an hour ago. But he knew he wouldn't be able to take her gently. He'd waited so long, fantasized about the cherry red mouth of hers far too many nights, to take her gently when he was this aroused. He needed her wet and ready, her body pleading for his cock no matter how hard he slammed into her. He wanted to make her come. *Again.* His chest swelled at the thought she had trusted him, trusted his touch, enough to find release. It wasn't, he imagined, something she allowed very often.

When the last tremor passed through Bryce, he slid to the floor, moving in inches, stopping to kiss her shoulder, the inside bend of her elbow and her wrist. As he moved, he guided her so that she no longer ran the vertical length of the bed, but was positioned across its width, her bottom perched at its edge.

She pressed her knees tight together and he kissed those, too. He ran his hand along the underside of her thighs, stroking and massaging until he felt some give to her nervous resistance. When she finally parted her legs, he could smell just how hot she was. The aroma of her juices mingled with her body wash, the fragrance a sharp ruby grapefruit that bit at his cock and nipples. He wanted to dive in face first, licking and nibbling her to another climax.

Instead, he advanced on her slowly. He worked her thighs far enough apart that his shoulders filled the "V" of her legs. Her labia remained closed, but the translucent cream of her excitement glistened at the dividing line. He beaded at the sight of her, the mix of citrus and the sweet honey of her cunt making his nostrils flare in appreciation of her scent. Reaching behind him, he found the bundle of towels that held the razor and shaving cream. He unrolled one towel and coaxed Bryce into lifting her bottom long enough for him to slide the towel under her. He used the act to bring his face close to the silky triangle of hair. He felt her tense in anticipation and wondered if she was ready to let him kiss her there, too.

God, I hope so.

His biceps under her thighs, he wrapped his forearms up and around her hips, holding her in place as he ran his mouth and nose over her soft bush. Everything about her was lush and enticing. She squirmed and he looked up in time to see her draw her arms above her head, her hands fisting in the bedspread.

Smiling, he watched her across the rise of her mound as his tongue slid over the top split of her labia. She tensed, her breasts still as she waited to breathe again. He slid his tongue between her lips and lightly touched the spot at the very top of her clit's spine. She pulled more air into her body but didn't breathe out. Her breasts pushed higher at the intake. Their small forms took on a hard ripeness as they swelled with her excitement. The nipples drew tight, darkening in jealousy as he teased her lower body.

Slow, slow, slowly. He paced his tongue's assault down the length of her clit. Just as slowly, he brought it back up. He heard her breathe out, and then he licked her again.

"Walt…" She said his name softly, a hint of pleading and long denied hunger making her voice thick. "Please don't stop."

In control, he smiled against the press of her labia and rolled the hood of her clit between his tongue and top lip before answering her. She rolled with him, her hips and shoulders grinding in opposite directions on the mattress, the gyrations punctuated by a low, frustrated mewling.

"I won't, Bryce baby," he answered. "I'm going to kiss and suck and tease until you come." He underscored his words with a quick swipe. "And then I'm going to shave you." Another lick, longer than the last and ending with a lingering suck. "And then I'm going to taste you all over again."

Bryce responded with a shaky moan, bringing her braceleted hand down to cover her face. He saw that all but a single charm—a dove—had been removed. Seeing Aphrodite's symbol of pure love, his chest tightened. Had Bryce put the charm on for him, knowing what it meant?

Diaz pushed aside that particular hope and concentrated on pleasing her. He brought both hands to her pussy, taking one full lip in each and massaging them. He used the pads of his thumbs to tease her, one rubbing against the inner breach of her clit while the other circled the tight ring of her cunt. Bryce continued to move with him, arching and thrusting her hips. Covering her engorged clit with his mouth and sucking at it, he used both thumbs to test the taut inner circle of muscle that guarded her pussy.

He teased her pussy wider, slicking his tongue down and inside her, licking his way back up to attack the swollen little hood while his thumbs pumped deeper. He whispered his vespers against the creamy silk of her labia and thighs.

"Wet. Hot. Ride it, Bryce."

She came as he urged her on. Only his hands touched her now. His thumbs stretched her wide and thrust into her while his index fingers rubbed up and down the length of her clit. Biting the flesh of her wrist, she bucked against the assault, pumped against his thumbs while her shoulders and head thrashed along the center of the bed.

He didn't stop until he'd wrung the last of her climax from her. Until his hands were wet with her cream and she was gently crying "no more".

Chapter Seven

Bryce wasn't sure about the shake in Diaz's hand as he brought the razor up to her shaving-cream covered mound. He was trying to control it, she could tell, but his efforts only intensified the shake until he trembled from his fingertips to his shoulder. His gaze was clouded and he obviously was trying just as hard to focus.

"Are you sure you don't want me to do this?" she asked.

"You'll go hide in the bathroom if I say 'yes'," he answered. His voice somehow managed to simultaneously shake and growl. It was the sexiest sound she had ever heard, and it tugged at her nipples and clit like one sharp pull on a drawstring.

"And if I promise I won't go hide?" She gave him a shy smile, not quite believing the teasing tone she had adopted was really hers or that she was contemplating shaving in front of him.

Diaz rubbed his cheek against the inside of her thigh, his gaze never leaving her face. "Bryce, I'm probably going to bust either way."

She giggled, pleased and shocked—shocked not only by what he said, but that he could make her giggle like some pre-teen. Strike that, she hadn't giggled since she was five, right before she'd started kindergarten.

"If you sit in the chair and watch," she suggested as she pushed up onto her elbows and took the razor from him, "you'll be able to use both hands to keep..." Arching one brow, she stared at the heavy bulge of erect cock that pressed against the front panel of his pants. "Keep *things* in control. Right?"

He nodded, looking even more dazed and unfocused, and reached for the bowl of water. He placed the bowl on the nightstand and repositioned the chair so that he could sit between her splayed legs.

"Ready?" She planted a foot on each side of him and gave the razor a little twirl, feeling naughty and completely in command of the situation.

Diaz clasped her ankles. She stared at him, the intensity of his grip surprising her. He licked his lips, then drew the bottom one between his teeth. He held her like that, his passion hypnotizing her, until he nodded.

Bryce drew the razorblade down across her mound. She rinsed the blade then stroked the same path again, the pale white skin of her mound appearing in a one-and-a-half inch stripe. Diaz let go of her left ankle and slid his hand beneath the waistband of his pants. She saw the push of fabric as he wrapped his hand around his cock and squeezed. It wouldn't be long, she realized, before her own hands began to shake. She wanted to see him—to touch, kiss and taste him as intimately as he had feasted upon her.

While she could still control her hands, she shaved a second stripe clean, and then a third. Diaz closed his eyes and leaned his head back. His lips, pressed tightly together, trembled as if he were biting at the insides. She stopped, giving them both time to regain their control. When he dropped his head back down, his gaze half-lidded, she continued clearing the strips that bordered the "V" of her mound. Shaving lower, she had to bring her feet up onto the chair's widely spaced armrests. She could feel the lips of her pussy part. Next came the cool onrush of air against the opening of her cunt as she totally exposed her body to his view. Diaz groaned, blinking every few seconds, both hands down his pants.

Pinching one labia to the side to shave its edge, she paused. "Show me," she said and tilted her chin in the direction of his lap.

"S-show you?" He was breathing hard, the smooth, muscled pectoral planes of his chest rising and falling in rapid succession.

Bryce gave the razor another twirl. "Yes, I want you as naked as I am," she answered and poised the razor over the exposed labia, refusing to go on until he complied.

Diaz gripped the waist of his pants, stretching the fabric past his erection as he eased them down his hips. Lifting his ass to push the pants down his thighs, his full cock came into view, and Bryce, made a soft gurgle at the back of her throat.

"Now I think I'm going to bust," she said, her gaze taking a second trip along the length of his uncut cock.

The tip was a watermelon center hidden inside a thick sheath of foreskin the color of light walnut. The veins bulged with his excitement and patterned the sheath with a network of bumps and ridges that left Bryce squirming in anticipation of having him inside her. He kicked out of the pants and the shaft jumped toward her. She wanted to reach out and wrap her hand around it—or hands, the girth and length not easily managed with just one. It was the most beautiful cock she had ever seen and the first one in the flesh.

Naked, muscles rippling with his physical confidence, Diaz leaned back against the chair and wrapped both hands around his cock. He pulled the foreskin down, revealing the shiny red arrowhead. Little pearl beads glistened in its slit, and Bryce licked her lips, her whole body churning for a taste.

Setting the razor on the towel Diaz had spread beneath her, she wiped the last of the shaving cream from her mound. Then she dropped both feet to the floor and leaned forward. "This isn't fair, you know?" she said.

She wasn't looking at his face. She'd had seven months to study it. His nose was cat-like—somewhat flat and broadening to a rounded tip. The jaw and cheekbones were strong, the chin a perfect curve that matched the fuller lower lip. The top lip was thinner, and oh-so-firm—able, as she had just learned, to exert exquisite pressure on the top length of her clit while his tongue and bottom lip gently teased the fleshy hood and the sensitive opening to her urethra. And she had gotten lost, if only for a few seconds, in the olive green gaze every time she'd come face-to-face with him since he'd moved in.

No, she knew that face and would always know it. Now she was looking at his cock, memorizing the lacework of thick veins and the plump tip that looked like an inverted strawberry, but undoubtedly tasted ten times better.

"Not fair?" He was stroking it now, using both hands to move the foreskin and rest of the sheath along the heavy shaft, the swollen tip momentarily winking out of sight before he smoothed it back into view.

"Not fair at all," she answered and planted the tip of her tongue against the center of her top lip. "I want a taste. I want...a drink."

■■■

Her mouth was small, a little heart of desire. Too small, most likely, but Walt was sure Bryce would only have to suck the tip into her before he exploded. He stood up, a little dizzy from all the blood diverted to his pounding cock. He took his time rising from the chair. He didn't want to rouse the old Bryce, who would have bolted the instant she landed on his patio.

"You look a little nervous," Bryce said.

Her hazel eyes had darkened to a smoky emerald and she seemed half in a trance. Not unfitting, he thought, snake charmer that she was. "I *am* nervous," he said.

Her gaze flicked down to his cock and then back up to his face. "I'll give it back, I promise."

She made a little scout's honor sign with her right hand, her braceleted hand sneaking beneath the pillow at the headboard. Walt wanted to believe that she was crossing her fingers beneath the pillow, unbinding herself from the promise even as she coaxed him closer to those juicy red lips.

"I didn't think you'd let me paint you," he said, stopping at the edge of the mattress, his cock even with her head. "I didn't think you'd come back this evening or let me...let me have you in any of the ways I wanted you."

She shook her head, as if she found his worries absurd. Wrapping her hand around his cock, she closed her eyes for an instant, exploring the shaft's length and shape by touch alone. She opened her eyes and looked up at him. "Put your hand in my hair," she said.

Walt ran his fingers through the honey-blonde hair, focusing hard on the combination of colors and shades that made up the total effect. It was his favorite color, to be found time and again in the paintings of his favorite artists. Bryce was the first woman he'd ever seen whose honey coloring was natural.

When she brought her tongue to the slit of his cock and sucked at the beads of pre-cum, he fisted his hand in all that glorious hair. "It's n-not going to take long," he warned. He wondered how much tighter his balls could get and then she brought her other hand up between his spread legs to stroke his heavy, cum-laden sacs.

Okay, tighter is possible, he thought, and drew in a deep breath.

She feather-stroked his perineum before returning to gently cup his balls at the same time her petite mouth stretched itself over the head. He added a second quick draw of air to the last, still unable to exhale. Finding another, new layer of tightness in his body, he grabbed her shoulder to keep from pumping past those sweet cherried lips and coming down her throat.

But she seemed to want him to do that, her touch goading him on. Her tongue flicked against one of the bulging veins that fed the tip of his erection. Her nails, soft but threatening, traveled his perineum again and stroked the top of his thighs and the skin of his balls before she cupped them. She held him like that, the knuckle of one index finger rubbing lightly at the base of his balls while she kept him wrapped tight in her mouth, her other hand stroking the part of the shaft she couldn't suck in.

His palm curled around the back of her head and he knew the fingertips of his other hand were digging into her shoulder. When he tried to relax his grip, she only sucked him harder, her mouth rising up and off his cock head before slurping back down. His thighs started trembling and he let go of her head to grip the edge of the nightstand.

"Bryce, baby, if you don't stop now, I'm going to come in your mouth."

Not skipping a beat, she sucked harder, her mouth descending lower and lower as she angled her head to accept more of his thick cock. Walt was dying looking at her, at her voracious appetite, her appreciation of his cock, at the strands of her silky hair rubbing against his thighs while her lips grew redder and wetter with the pleasure of bringing him to climax. There was no time to warn her again as he released the nightstand and took her head between his hands. Arching into the sweet center of her mouth, he cried her name once and came.

Chapter Eight

Having finally surrendered her hold on the delicious red knob of his cock head, Bryce fell onto her back and watched Diaz collapse into the chair. He was breathing through his mouth and looked more than a little dazed. Seeing him vulnerable like that, she wanted to descend on him once more, but licked her lips instead. She still tasted his cum and the slightly sharp taste surprised her. She had read that its substance was mostly sugar.

"I didn't realize it was that nice," she said, her body relaxed and sleepy.

"Hmmmm?"

Bryce pressed her eyes shut, horrified she'd said it aloud. She felt a blush warm her skin. Damn, what would he think if he realized she was a total newb when it came to actually having a partner during sex?

"Bryce, baby, what did you just say?"

She cleared her throat, not opening her eyes when she answered. "I said that was nice."

"That wasn't quite what you said."

His tender and curious tone practically demanded that she look at him. She turned her head, her quick gaze noting that, even without the erection, his cock was solidly plump and long. Pulling her gaze up to his equally handsome face, she gave a tentative smile before confessing. "I just hadn't done that before."

"Ah," he said and nodded, but then his apparent satisfaction with her answer evaporated and his expression twisted with a new confusion. "Uhm...what part of 'that' do you mean? I mean, all of it...or just the last bit?"

"All of it." *And more,* she thought. Everything was new—his kissing her...

And that other kiss. She sighed inwardly as she remembered his mouth moving lower, and how his kisses there had left her shaking and with stars dancing behind her shut eyelids.

"Oh, god, Bryce, I'm so sorry. I didn't realize— wouldn't have..." He fell silent, his body pressed hard against the back of his chair as if he were trying to run or hide.

She rolled until she was on her side and facing him. "Don't be sorry," she said, and lightly touched his knee. "I'm not really much of an innocent—just my mouth was a virgin."

Diaz let out a shaky breath and nodded. She couldn't tell if he was relieved or disappointed or somewhere in between. What would he think if he knew the whole truth?

Leaning forward, he clasped her hand and brought it to his lips. He smiled as he kissed the back of her fingers. "Didn't mean to spaz on you," he said. "Just the thought that maybe you hadn't been with another man—that I should have gone much slower..."

Unable to keep the pretense up, she dropped her gaze. His grip on her hand tightened but she refused to look up. She couldn't look at him. Damn, why did she have to start crying now?

"Brycie, you *have* been with another man, right?" Diaz moved to the bed. Laying beside her, he tried to cradle her but she kept twisting away. Reaching an arm across her, he scooped up part of the bedspread and pulled until she was trapped flat against his chest. "Brycie, have you?"

She shook her head "no". It felt good to have his arms around her, but that only made her want to cry more and she shook her head again. It would only take a few more questions and he'd realize he'd let a freak into his apartment.

"Bryce, has a man been with you?"

She had to stop and think about the change in a question she had already answered. "No, nothing like that, who would want—"

"I want you, dammit." His voice sounded a little angry and frustrated as all hell.

Too bad all that passion would evaporate Sunday at midnight, when the extended ball was over and she turned back into a fat little pumpkin.

"So you—you took care of it yourself?" Diaz rolled Bryce onto her back, holding the sides of her face so that she would have been looking at him if she wasn't still refusing to open her eyes.

Bryce nodded, chewing at her bottom lip while she waited for whatever muse-created spell that held him to snap and break.

"How old were you?"

"Tw-twenty three." Damn, why did he insist on prolonging this!

He remained poised over her, his body feeling to her as if it was locked in thought. She couldn't open her eyes to see if his expression held any trace of what he was thinking. She would, if she had to, walk from the room with her eyes closed. Seeing his face twist with the reality of the day would kill her.

"Brycie, that's an awful lot of time to make up for," he said at last. "And you're only giving me the weekend to do it?"

She would give him forever, if that's what he wanted. But, instead of telling him that, she lied. "Yes."

When Diaz was quiet for a long while, she finally opened her eyes.

"You will recant, Miss Schoene," he said, his sumptuous mouth erupting in a broad grin. He moved down her body, kissing and sucking. Light bruises flushed her skin, marking his path. When he reached the line of hair she hadn't finished shaving, he stopped and pulled lightly at it with his lips and then warned her, "Because the kid gloves are off as of right now."

Cock erect once more, Diaz ordered Bryce back onto the towel with her body horizontally across the bed. He knelt on the floor in front of her spread legs and dispensed a small puff of shaving cream into his hand. He lathered the cream onto the still unshaven lips of her pussy and picked up the razor. His strokes were soft and short, but diligent. He interrupted his work with frequent kisses to her thighs and calves.

When he was all done, he wiped the shaving cream residue away and left to get fresh water. He cleaned her a second time. She could feel him making her skin all pink and fresh, from the freshly shaven mound to the inner folds of her labia. But every stroke of the washcloth only seemed to make her slicker.

Diaz wrapped the razor and shaving cream into the spare towel and picked up the bowl. Bryce lifted up to pull the second towel from beneath her, but he shook his head.

"Leave it, Brycie," he warned. "I'm not done yet."

He left the room and she waited, her body tense while she guessed at the origin of the sounds coming from the other side of the apartment. She could hear the refrigerator door opening, the sound of ice cubes bouncing in glasses and the solid "thunk" of a knife hitting the flat surface of a wooden cutting board over and over. There was the faint pop of a cork and liquid sloshing against the glass and ice. He returned to the room a few seconds later, using the cutting board as an impromptu tray.

Bryce pushed up onto her elbows. Glasses and a cut lemon. The two short glasses held a rich amber brown liquid on the rocks. Diaz passed her one and she knew from the smell what it was. *Courvoisier.* She'd only had it once before, at a friend's divorce celebration—a large portion of the first month's alimony check blown on three bottles consumed over the weekend by half a dozen very drunk young women.

She dipped just the tip of her tongue into the glass and then ran it over her lips. Fruity, orange with a taste of apricot and pear. More flavors teased her as the first impression faded. A hint of chocolate and vanilla, and sweet spices that she couldn't name from a baker's rack.

"You can savor the next glass," Diaz said and tossed his back with one sacrilegious swallow. "The first one's just a brace."

"A brace?" The question shook a little as it left her and she held the glass more firmly.

He nodded and picked up the cut lemon. When he ran it over his lips, Bryce followed his earlier example and downed the rest of her drink. She'd never seen a gaze so wicked or hot.

Feeling the slow burn of the cognac as it traveled down her throat, she gave a little puff. "You're not a nice man," she said. But then a purely nice man would not have shouldered his way past all her defenses—muse or no muse.

Taking Bryce's glass, he fished an ice cube out and sank on his knees in front of her—one hand holding the lemon, the other the Courvoisier-covered ice cube. Starting at the top of her freshly shaven mound, he slid the lemon over her skin.

Hell! She took a deep breath, wanting to squeal at the sharp burn of citrus. But then Diaz blew on the area and followed it with the ice cube. The heat that followed was different. The Courvoisier mellowed it. And then his tongue, licking at the melt water, soothed the last of the hurt. She relaxed and he repeated the pattern, moving over the full expanse of her mound. She arched to meet his mouth each time he blew or ran his tongue over her to erase the sting of liquor and lemon.

When he reached her pussy lips, he put the lemon aside and scooped a fresh cube from the glass. He was moving sinfully slow, igniting the burn and then fueling it with soft puffs of air before he licked it away. Burning hot, ice cold, wet licks, he hadn't even reached her inner folds and his erotic torment had her on the verge of coming.

When he parted her lips, she was sure she would pass out. He ran the cube over her clit, his tongue thrusting into her cunt as he did so. Spooning her juices with his tongue, he laved them over her clit and then sucked them off before swiping the ice cube along the stiff line of her pussy once more. Another tongue-full of cream and then he was sucking at her clit.

Pulling away, he rocked back on his heels, one hand holding her open while he teased the ring of her pussy with the ice. "Brycie, you're drenched, baby."

And only getting wetter.

She moaned, thrusting with her hips until the cube and his two fingers penetrated. It was cold and melting fast. She could feel him V-ing her open with his fingers and using his tongue to push the ice cube deeper into her cunt. Then he fucked her like that, his tongue and fingers pushing and stretching into the tight walls of her pussy while the spreading chill from the cube made her clamp down and push back. She felt the melt water leave her, trickling down her perineum and teasing her ass. The cold made her tighter, made everything about her harder. Her nipples were at full attention, aching from the soft flow of air through the room.

His tongue flicking inside her and around the trembling circle of her cunt provided a warm contrast. Tight but sloppy wet, cold but warm, the sensations collided against one another—shattered along her nerves. Bryce spread her legs in a silent demand for more. He had been two fingers thick inside her, now he was three, maybe four, wide as he finger fucked her. He worked deeper into her cunt, his mouth moving up to tease her clit with a sustained and hard sucking. She rode him, her thrusts feral. Panting and squeezing down on his fingers, she held his head tight to her pussy with one hand while she bit into the palm of the other. But when she came, she couldn't stop the scream.

Chapter Nine

Diaz rose to his feet. His not-so-little soldier stood at attention, so rigid and ready for service she half expected it to salute her. Diaz, on the other hand, had a slightly wild look to him and he ran a shaking hand across his smooth face. He looked at the nightstand's single drawer but shook his head in dismissal. And then a "Eureka!" expression came over his face and he spun around to the double sliding-door closet. He pulled the left door to the side and Bryce saw that the top shelf was stacked with boxes and he had a column of them running against the side wall. Words like "bedroom" and "misc" were scrawled on them in red marker.

The sight of his muscled ass and back teased her as he stretched to pull the first box of miscellany down. He tore the top flaps back, rummaged through the contents and then plopped the box down and reached for a second one. More pawing was followed by an excited "yes!". He fished a smaller package out and shoved the box back on the top shelf.

He turned and Bryce saw that he had an unopened box of condoms. She felt her jaw go slack. Not only did it mean that he was intent on filling her with that glorious cock, but that box had—most likely—been there since he'd moved in. Did that mean he'd been celibate for the last seven months? The thought that she wasn't the only one with a lot of lost time to make up for had her reaching for him as he approached the bed.

She wanted to take him in her mouth again and tease him with the cubes the same way he had teased her. She pictured running the ice around the tip of his cock and down its length. Then she'd lick him until he came in her mouth once more. But he seemed thoroughly intent on having something else right now. He had left Bryce placed across the width of the bed and he took the towel from beneath her bottom. Tearing open the condom's wrapper, he gestured with his head for her to move back up the bed.

He unrolled the latex sheath onto his cock and then climbed onto the mattress. He pushed Bryce's legs wider apart, but didn't plunge straight into her. Instead, he dipped two fingers into her center, coating them in the rich cream that flowed from her cunt. He rubbed his fingers over her clit, fast and then slow, then fast again. Slowing once more, he took the swollen hood of her clit between his knuckles and rolled it while his thumb teased the raw slit below. Only once her hips were rolling with him did he bring the head of his cock to rest against the entrance to her pussy.

He pushed in, changed the angle of his approach with a slide of his hips, and pushed deeper. With their chests pressed together, Diaz buried his face in the bend of her neck.

"I can't wait for the day you let me in uncovered, Brycie." He punctuated his words with deep, undulating strokes.

Splaying her fingers, Bryce covered his ass cheeks, holding on for dear life as his muscles flexed, twisted and rolled beneath her hand. Every little movement brought him deeper inside her. His cock head was kneading the bulb of nerves high up in her cunt, each new press making her curl tighter around him. She moaned and tried for a few fractions of a second to imagine how it could possibly feel any better.

He was all the way in her now, and he was so thick. Unimaginably tight with her own need, she could feel every layer of their love making. The condom barely moved inside her despite the deep strokes he took. Beneath that layer, the veined sheath slid back and forth. Even deeper, more at his center, the full glory of his erection moved. The ample head traveled beneath condom and foreskin, creating ripples within ripples. Each time the head passed beneath one of the thick veins, massaging that knot of pleasure, Bryce moaned and ground harder against him.

Diaz lifted off her, just enough that he could increase the pressure of his strokes and knead one of her swollen breasts. His hand covered her completely, the fingers cupping and squeezing the breast's ripe hardness. He pulled the nipple taut, stretching it tighter and tighter until she arched up, her climax slamming through her in one long shudder.

She collapsed against the bed and he fell with her, just as he had promised earlier in the night. Wrapping his arms around her, he hugged her tightly to him. He kept thrusting—continued filling and fucking her until he went completely motionless. She heard him grind his teeth and then felt the first jerk of his cock as he started to come. A second and a third thrust and ripple followed as he filled the condom. Bryce gasped, the sensation of his climax and the fierce way he held on triggering another orgasm within her.

Diaz pulled out and rolled to the edge of the bed. He held his hand against his chest in an apparent attempt to restart his heart or slow his breathing. She couldn't tell which. After a few more seconds, he moved onto his side, his back to her, and she heard the scrape of him dragging the small garbage can next to the nightstand closer. He threw the spent condom away, clicked the floor lamp off and then rolled back to Bryce. In one final motion, he pulled the bedspread across both their bodies and trapped her in his arms.

She lifted her head enough to see the clock and know that the time was closing in on midnight. That gave her just forty-eight more hours. But she felt too sleepy and content to worry about the quickly dwindling time she had with him.

She put her hand on one of his sculpted biceps and stroked it with her thumb. "You didn't get much sketching done," she said.

"Bryce, I'm going to remember everything about you for the rest of my life," he answered, the sound of his voice telling her he was just as fatigued and relaxed. "I've got years to paint you—but only this weekend to love you."

Bryce stopped stroking his arm, her body motionless within its circle. Had he just said he only had the weekend to "love" her? Surely that was just a turn of phrase? He couldn't be in love with her.

"Walt?" She said his name quietly.

He answered her with the soft whistle of a snore.

☒ ☒ ☒

At six in the morning, Bryce finally gave up on trying to fall asleep for more than twenty minutes at a time and climbed from Diaz's bed. Getting out of it without waking him wasn't easy. He'd spent the night spooned against her, an arm across her shoulder or around her waist, his body slightly curled so that his lips were pressed against her neck or shoulder. The way he held her like that felt a little possessive. She found it both slightly annoying and completely wonderful. Any annoyance she'd felt disappeared once she'd finally extracted herself from his sleeping embrace. Watching him from the end of the bed, she felt a small pang of need and was tempted to crawl back under the covers and feel his strong arms wrap instantly around her.

Instead of returning to bed, she retrieved the lovely outfit and gold strapped sandals Erato had forced on her. She headed into Diaz's bathroom to change before going home. She would, she decided, borrow his keys while he slept and slip next door for a shower, fresh clothes and some makeup. He certainly couldn't see her like she was, she thought, opening the bathroom door and flipping the light switch on.

She almost jumped straight from her skin at the sight of Erato perched on the edge of the tub. Bryce shut the door, grabbed a towel to cover herself and turned on the bathroom fan before she acknowledged the muse. "What the hell are you doing in his apartment!"

"Making sure you don't do anything stupid, dear."

"It's a little too late for that, don't you think?" She opened the carefully folded clothes with a hard snap. "Now get out of here so I can dress."

"No can do," Erato answered and stretched her long legs out. She tilted back over the tub, a superior grin on her otherwise lovely face.

Bryce took a second to examine the tub. It was an original fixture to the old apartment building, cast iron, luxuriously deep and perched atop small pieces of metal that resembled animal paws. The tub was definitely deep enough to drown the muse in—which would be satisfying but pointless if Erato truly were an immortal. There was also a shower curtain suspended from an oval rod attached to the ceiling and an add-on showerhead with its flexible metal hose hooked to the faucet at the tub's side. Both the hose and curtain would be good for strangling an annoying muse. Again, pointless, but at least the need would be out of her system for as long as it took Erato to speak again.

"Oh, nice," Erato said, her voice dry and disdainful. "Fact is, you get back in that apartment of yours, into the shower that faces the mirror...the mirror you try every morning not to look in...you might not come back. Then our little deal is blown and I've wasted a perfectly good evening."

She paused, a nostalgic smile lighting an expression that had grown harrid. "But he does have one of the most beautiful uncut cocks I've ever seen."

"Y-you're a perv," Bryce blurted out. "You were watching? All of it?"

"Don't get the panties you're not wearing in a knot, dear." Erato laughed and took the outfit from her. "A large part of inspiration is observation. How do you think a muse helps a shut-in like you without going out and seeing what other people are doing?"

"A shut-in?" Bryce wasn't sure which was worse, that Erato had watched them last night or that she was calling Bryce names. "I most certainly am not!"

"Oh, sure, sure," Erato started, holding up a hand and clicking off the pattern of Bryce's weeks. "You go to classes on Tuesday and Thursday, you teach G.E.D. students Monday and Wednesday evening—both on the same campus and in the same building. You go to the grocery store on your way to or from campus. You do ninety percent of your bill paying and non-grocery shopping online. You recently stopped going out to meals with your friends—and you can't expect them to keep asking much longer when all they ever get now is a 'No thank you'. Are you going to come back here and eat breakfast with him, when you've all but stopped eating in front of friends you've had for years?"

"How do you know all this?" Bryce clutched the towel around her body. She felt like the last year of her life had just been placed under a microscope, and it left her at least as exposed as she had been while splayed in front of Diaz. She tried to think of the last time she'd gone out with friends. Had it really been that long?

Erato stood up. Her large hands framed the sides of Bryce's face and she planted a motherly kiss on Bryce's forehead. "Because I know you now, and so I know everything about you. It's part of a muse's job—well, at least for the permanent hires. You're still working on a strict need-to-know basis, dear—that's why you can't see into his mind the way I can see into yours."

Cocking her head, Erato listened for a second beyond the noise of the fan. "Why wouldn't you eat in front of him, anyway...you were holding him in your mouth last night."

Bryce shook her head—it was totally different. "You've seen him, he's perfect."

Erato's gaze drifted back to Bryce and she shrugged. "Perfection is relative, dear. You've never been to Olympus." She stopped again and moved closer to the bathroom door. "And you've never been one of the girls the Perfect Mr. Diaz let mommy chase away."

"Mommy?" Bryce asked, but Erato disappeared just as Diaz knocked on the bathroom door.

Damn, she should have changed in front of Erato and left before he had a chance to wake up. Hiding most of her body behind the door, she unlocked and opened it a few inches to peek out at him. He was barefoot and shirtless, having only slipped his pants back on. "Did I wake you?" she asked.

Brow furrowed, he angled his head to the side and then glanced at the mirror that hung over the double sink. "I heard conversation."

Bryce's gaze widened as she thought through how she was going to explain. Give him the truth and he would think she was crazy—but he'd likely think the same thing if she said she talked to herself. Which she did, anyway. A lot.

"Story...uhm, that I have to turn in Monday, not done yet," she explained. "The class is pass or fail based on the story, and I was trying out some dialogue."

"Monday?" The deep lines smoothed a little, but he still looked concerned. "I don't want to make you fail the class. It's your last semester, isn't it?"

"Oh, no, don't worry." She waved her hand, and the door opened another few inches. "I just need to tweak some things and such...that bit of dialogue especially." She hesitated, wincing. "You didn't hear any of it, did you?"

Diaz shook his head. "Do you want to run it by me?"

He looked serious, as if he didn't think she was lying, and Bryce smiled. "No, I'd like to keep how much I suck at writing between me and the professor."

He nodded and then motioned in the direction of the sinks' counter. "You went to your apartment already?"

Ready to remind him that she'd worn the dress before, Bryce turned her head just in time to find a black georgette blouse paired with black sandals and silk pants. Next to the outfit was a travel kit. The patterned swirls of pink and cream, edged with an antique gold ribbon made the kit too feminine to belong to Diaz. *Damn that muse!*

"Yeah, I borrowed your keys," she improvised. "I hope you don't mind?" At least the weekend would improve her lying skills.

"No, I'm just glad you were back when I woke up," he answered, his hand on the doorknob like he wanted her to let him the rest of the way in. "I would have felt abandoned."

Bryce snorted at the thought—she certainly hadn't intended running off, just catching a quick shower. She wanted every last minute the weekend would offer despite Erato's arguments to the contrary. "Come on," she teased. "You really expect me to believe that? Who in her right mind would leave you?"

The second the question left her mouth, she wished she could call it back. His face took on a distant look that he quickly masked, and she wondered whether he was thinking of another woman or the fact that she had told him she would only give him this weekend?

"Well," he said, his good humor apparently returning. "The key phrase in there is 'right mind', isn't it?"

She nodded and he changed the subject to yet another one she didn't want to discuss.

"I've never seen that outfit before, either."

It certainly wasn't something she would have worn before this weekend, she agreed silently. Although the idea of wearing it for him excited her. Beyond its classic black elegance, it was a little sexy. It was cut in a low curve at the top that would leave the top of her shoulders bare. A drawstring tie looked like it would fall just below her breasts to accentuate them. From that drop point, the lower half flowed in soft voluminous folds that would end even with her thigh line and hide the fact her body grew wider the further south one's gaze traveled. With both the top and bottom in black, she knew the overall effect would be slimming. The georgette material would keep the dark color tolerable if they ventured out into the August heat.

"My aunt bought it for me." Another lie and she smiled, realizing it was easier to fib the closer you were to the actual truth. "A very, very, very old aunt," Bryce amended. "It's kind of sad, really. She lives with eight cats—and I'm her only living relative. But it's not exactly something I can wear to campus, so it's been sitting in my closet since Christmas."

Picking the top up, she winced as a pin stuck her. *Bloody muses! No sense of humor when the joke was on them. But a mere mortal was fair game for their amusement.*

She pulled the pin out and showed him her bloodied finger tip. "I'm surprised the tags aren't attached still."

"Well, I'm very...very...very glad you pulled it out of the closet for me," he teased. "Why don't I make us some breakfast while you shower," he offered before immediately asking, "Unless I can come in and wash your back?"

The offer was tempting. She certainly wanted to see him nude again—as soon as possible. But Erato had been right, yesterday's self-consciousness was back. She didn't want to have breakfast with him or have him see her in the shower, completely sans makeup and with the hair he seemed to like so much turned into a wet and tangled mess. She would shower alone, put on the exquisite outfit Erato had provided her with, and hopefully find that the muse had been equally considerate in stocking the travel kit with makeup.

"I think," she started shyly, "I want you to make breakfast while I clean up. Now, if I come out and find you naked and offering yourself up as a serving dish, that would be even better."

Diaz winked, as if he was more than ready to take her up on the dare. Before she could tell him she'd been joking, he saluted and quickly pulled the door shut. She stared at the door for a second while she pondered whether she should call him back and make it clear she had only been teasing.

Hell, eating breakfast in front of him was going to be hard enough—but off of him, as well?

Chapter Ten

Relaxing beneath the hot water, Bryce convinced herself Diaz had only been joking. He'd have cereal or eggs and sausage cooked up, and she'd eat a little bit while he ate all of his. Not that she couldn't easily imagine eating a bite or two of sausage from his body. She could almost taste the flavor of it on his skin, meat stacked on meat. Or, she decided and eased further into the fantasy, maybe she would prefer a pulpy dribble of fruit across the rippled muscles of his stomach. She could definitely imagine licking a line of juice up the thick forward jut of his cock.

Out of the shower, her hair drying while she applied makeup, Bryce gave her lips a slow lick. That would definitely be the best breakfast she could think of. She slipped into the top and pants, thankful that Erato had at least seen fit to provide her with panties this time. Without panties, it would only take her a few seconds of being around Diaz before her excitement soaked through the silk pants.

When she opened the bathroom door, she didn't see Diaz immediately. She walked toward the galley-sized kitchen and saw the cutting board and frying pan in the sink. Heading toward the bedroom, she heard him clear his throat and turned to find him stretched out on the couch, naked but for the food covering him.

"I was joking," she whispered, gaze wide as it traveled from the kiwi slices covering his nipples to the pared strawberries in a line down to his navel before finally reaching the smiley face of sausage patties. A plate half full with the same food sat on the coffee table

"Too late," he said. He held a peeled banana in his hand and he broke it in half. "Come and kiss me," he said and then stuck a piece of banana between his lips.

Bryce slowly shook her head and he pulled the banana back out.

"I'll starve if you don't," he said.

Kneeling on the floor next to him, she studied the spread again. "I thought you were an artist?" she challenged. He looked at her like she'd just impugned his manhood, but it wasn't his lovely cock that had her biting back a giggle. "Oh, don't pout...you have to admit it," she teased. "Except for the center piece, that's the most ridiculous smiley face ever!"

"Then you'll have to make it disappear," he said, flexing his abdominal muscles so that his cock bobbed in her direction.

She arched one brow and ran a fingertip over his erection. "You mean the centerpiece?"

"That, too," he answered and popped the banana back in his mouth.

Bryce slid along the floor until she was even with his head. She pulled her hair out of the way and leaned over his face to gingerly take a bite of the banana. He worked an equal bite into his mouth and winked at her. He loosened the drawstring on her blouse then dropped his hand to her hip. She shared another bite with him while his hand traveled under the hem of her blouse and then up to cup her bare breast. He gave a little pinch to her nipple and she moaned, biting through the banana and finding his lips. She swallowed the slick bite whole and then kissed him. Her tongue slid into his mouth and he drew her nipple taut, releasing her breast only when she drew back for air.

"Strip," he ordered. "Here, completely."

"I won't get messy," she promised before picking up one of the kiwi slices and bringing it to his mouth. He kept his lips pressed together and when she gently ran the slice over his lips he turned his head to the side. She bit into the fruit, watching him play hard to get while she finished the slice. "I said I won't get messy," she repeated.

"But I plan on you getting very messy," he answered.

Bryce stood, biting on her lip to control the pout she could feel building. She stepped from the pants and underwear first, leaving her body partially camouflaged by the top's length. She folded the clothes and sat them on the coffee table before kneeling again. She untied the drawstring the rest of the way. Pressed against the side of the couch, she pulled the blouse off, tossed it on top of the folded pants, and dipped her head to take another kiwi slice from his chest. This time, when she offered it to him, he took a bite.

Still holding the piece of fruit in his mouth, he cupped her breast and drew her to him. With the kiwi between his teeth, he rubbed against her nipple until it was taut and glistening with the fruit's juices. Then he swallowed the kiwi and began sucking at her nipple.

The way he sucked at her made Bryce instantly melt. First he pulled the nipple all the way into his warm, wet mouth. Then his lips circled her areola and he stroked one side of the bud with the flat of his tongue. Slow, sweet—it made her feel like she was floating. When he was finished with being soft and sweet, he increased the pressure, stretching the tip until the sharp pull of pleasure shattered across her skin and he finally released her.

She bent to pluck a strawberry slice from his chest, but he popped one in his mouth and drew her back to take a bite. As she chewed, he took another fat chunk and drizzled a trail of juice between her breasts, down her stomach and across her mound. He slid the tip between her labia, rubbing her clit with it before he popped the strawberry into his mouth and swallowed. He crooked his finger at her, motioning her close enough that he could lick the line of juice between her breasts while his fingers parted her labia again to caress and tug at her clit.

Except for the fact that his mouth, tongue and fingers were teasing her bare skin, Bryce forgot she was naked.

She pushed him flat onto his back with one hand and squeezed strawberry pulp up his chest, over his nipples and up to press against his closed lips. He smiled just enough for the juice to dribble into his mouth. She followed the juice with her tongue. When the taste was gone, she followed the trail she had left over his nipples, down to his navel and the first bite of meat. The quarter size sausage patty was still warm and juicy. She offered it to him and selected a second slice for her own use. She ran it over his erection, making his cock glisten a dark golden oak.

She placed all the slices on the nearby plate and took his cock in hand, smiling at him once before descending. "This is what I'm hungry for."

▨ ▨ ▨

Walt watched the red, wet pout of Bryce's lips swallow the head of his cock, the oils from the meat lubricating the way as she absorbed more of his shaft into her mouth. Her hair slid down the side of her face and blocked his view. He rose up on his elbows and tucked the strand behind her ear. He watched, absorbed in her movements and the sensations. But, as much as he loved her mouth working his shaft, wrapping him in its tight warm caverns, it wasn't what he had planned.

"Bryce," he panted, his fingers digging into the couch's leather cushions, "I'm supposed to be driving you crazy."

She suctioned him tighter, deeper, obviously intent on not letting him have his way just yet. There was something about the touch of her mouth that drove him quickly to the edge, faster than he had ever experienced before. And she was taking him all the way in now, her lower jaw pulling down to expand her throat and welcome the sensitive tip of his erection. He could feel her muscles contracting in protest. The convulsive squeezes of her throat were about to drive him insane. Trying to control himself, he held the couch cushions in a white-knuckled grip before he demanded too much of that near virgin mouth.

Bryce curled a palm around his hip and dug her fingertips into the side of his tensed glutes. Spreading her legs so that they were no longer tucked beneath her, she lowered her stomach and chest closer to the floor. She drew him onto his side and a little forward, so that his stiff cock pointed at an angle over the edge of the couch and her throat was in a straight line with her upturned mouth. Her other palm gripped his exposed shoulder. She held onto him like that, her body rigid everywhere but her shoulders, mouth and throat. He could feel her elongating her tongue, pressing it flat against the side of his cock.

Walt put a hand on her shoulder, gently forcing her first to release him and then into a position flat on her back. He slid onto the floor next to her and lifted the plate from the coffee table. There was a condom beneath it and he picked it up. He flashed the silver wrapper at Bryce but didn't open it. Instead, he put the package back on the table.

"I'm going to fill you until you come Bryce," he promised, the head of his cock poised at the threshold of her cunt. She groaned and he groaned with her, sliding hard and fast into her slick cunt.

Bryce clamped down on him, her pussy snug around the sensitive foreskin and sheath. She contracted at the base and the impish gleam in her eyes told him it was intentional. Walt threw his head back as she did it again.

"Christ, Brycie, what are you doing?" he moaned, tightening his ass cheeks and thrusting deeper into her.

"Kegels." She giggled as she answered, the word coming out as "kehegels." She tightened again, the smile on her face fixed and slightly maniacal. She was panting, determined. "I can get myself off just with the contractions," she confessed before blushing furiously.

"Ah...damn, Brycie, you're going to bring me off just as quick—if not quicker."

Her mouth twitched and she gave another concentrated roll and thrust of her hips. "I want you coming inside me," she said and gave him another squeeze that made his eyes roll back in their sockets.

Walt dropped his head, breathing harder, his legs and ass shaking with the effort not to come. He wanted to, wanted to come inside her unsheathed in an ultimate exchange of intimacy. "I'm not *covered*," he managed to grunt out.

"I'm covering you." Another squeeze of the muscles along her perineum and he dropped his body until it pressed against her.

"You could get pregnant." It sounded stupid warning her when it was against his self interest. His chest and cock swelled at the thought of her carrying his child.

"Then you'd have to marry me," she answered, her tone so matter-of-fact it startled him.

Walt pushed up until he could look down at her, his erection buried in her cock-hugging depths. She had her eyes closed, as if she didn't want him to see the truth of what she was thinking. But was it that she wanted something beyond this weekend as much as he did, or that she planned on giving him a complete brush off come Monday morning?

"Bryce," he whispered. "You can't joke about this—not about a baby."

She stilled beneath him and her eyes fluttered open. There was a flicker of scrutiny as if she wondered at the sudden source of panic in his voice. But then the look was gone, leaving the beautiful, soul-deep hazel eyes in thoughtful study of his face for another moment.

"If you get me pregnant, Walt Diaz, you'll have to marry me," she repeated. "Do you understand?"

Walt answered her with a kiss, his body melting as she rolled the muscles at the outer edge of her pussy along the base of his shaft. She was inching up and down him with just those muscles, pulling his sensitive sheath with her as she hugged him tighter with the rest of her cunt. He laid flat against her, nuzzling the side of her face as he let her control both of their bodies. The intimacy of being inside her like this brought him to the very edge of his climax. Despite one questionable claim from a previous partner, he didn't think he had ever climaxed inside a woman without a condom on. As far as his memory served—his sober memory, that was—he'd never dared to even venture into one of his earlier lovers without an interposing layer of latex. Here, nothing separated Bryce from him and every last inch of his cock experienced the way her sex hugged him.

Arching his back as she pulled him deeper, her little pants of "yes, now" goading him on, he came.

Calling her name.

Telling her he loved her.

Chapter Eleven

They rested quietly on the floor after their climax, the coffee table pushed far from the couch so that Diaz could lay on his side next to Bryce, one arm cradling her head while the other arm lay gently across her chest as he stroked her shoulder. He wanted to talk, she knew that, but every time he opened his mouth, she tensed on purpose.

It wasn't his fault he'd said it, and she didn't have any intention of holding him to it—or any other promise he had made. That wouldn't be fair, knowing what she knew. And she wouldn't get pregnant, at least not without divine intervention—the cocktail of birth control pills her doctor prescribed suddenly accomplishing more than just controlling her monthly cycle down to a non-event.

"I know what you're thinking," Diaz blurted out at last. "That I want to take what I said back, or brush it off like I didn't say it."

Bryce turned to him and placed her palm softly against his chest. "No, that isn't what I'm thinking," she answered. "I think you meant to say it—all of it. I think you still mean it."

"Then why do I get the feeling you were trying to shut me up?"

He rolled, forcing Bryce onto her back again and positioning himself over her. He cupped her cheek, his gaze studying her with an intensity that almost frightened her.

"Because I was," she answered.

Diaz pulled back. Before he sat up and turned his back to her, she saw a stone mask settle over his face. "You mean, it's because you didn't want to hear it?"

"No." She answered slowly, trying to choose her words very carefully and cursing Erato for putting her in a situation where she couldn't even acknowledge what she most wanted. "It felt wonderful hearing you say it."

She rolled onto one elbow and reached up, her fingertips brushing his shoulder blade. The muscle beneath twitched with his anger and she dropped her hand. "I just think the weekend's novelty will wear off for you, and so it hurts to hear you say it even knowing you mean it right now."

That was close enough to the truth, she thought, waiting tensely for him to respond. She didn't have to tell him she knew without a doubt that it would wear off. She could sense he was growing angrier, her answer only making things worse. This time, when she placed her hand against his back, he jerked entirely away from her.

"So you think I'm a shallow fuck, is that it?" he asked. He kept his back to her, his whole body wound tight.

Bryce sat up, placed her back to the couch and pulled her legs in close to her body. Damn, if Erato was going to give her words for the story, why couldn't she have given her words for this? "I think what I'm saying is that you have a little over a day and a half to change my world view."

Well, that shocked him, she thought as he turned to look at her, his gaze clouded with confusion.

"Change your world view?"

She nodded and swallowed hard before she answered. "That a man like you could ever love a woman like me."

She despised the hurt she could hear in her own voice but it seemed to melt his anger. He turned around and scooted until they were both sitting with their backs against the couch.

He put his arm behind her and pressed his lips to her ear. "Brycie, baby, who hurt you like this?"

Who hadn't? She shook her head, letting him know that she wouldn't answer. She had always been larger than other girls as far back as she could remember. What point was there in telling him about her first year in school and all the years that followed up to college, or about her parents' silent loathing? That was all in the past, or should be, and all subjective. At least that's what her intellect told her.

"I think you pegged it," she said, trying to joke. "Brycie, 'baby'."

"No." He held her chin between his thumb and index finger and lightly forced her to look at him. He kissed the edges of her mouth, whisper soft at first and then more insistent. "I only meant my baby, Bryce. Mine."

A hard kiss emphasized his claim and then he nervously pulled back. He ran a hand over his chest and offered a playful grimace at the feel of the tacky fruit juices. He looked in the direction of the bathroom and the grimace turned to a sheepish grin. "We're messy," he said.

"Just like you said we'd be." She smiled back, ready if he was to pretend for the rest of the weekend that this was more than a charade.

Diaz took her hand and led her into the bathroom where he filled the oversized tub with hot water and garnet-red bath salts scented with pomegranate. When it was a little over a third full, he tested to make sure it wasn't too hot. He took her left hand, holding her steady while he coaxed her into the bath. She sat down, relaxing her hold on him but he didn't let go.

"I'm in," she said and tried to pull her hand away.

Head tilted, he studied the charm bracelet. He ran it round until the clasp faced him, his grip on her hand tightening when she tugged sharply. "The heat might damage it," he said and unhooked the clasp. "And you seem so fond of it—I wouldn't want to see it broken."

A dark blue enamel box sat in the middle of the double sinks and he placed the bracelet inside it before climbing into the tub behind Bryce. When she wouldn't relax into him, he leaned against her back, his arms holding her just below the bottom swell of her breasts. He pulled her hair to the side, so that it hung over one shoulder and allowed his lips access to the opposite curve of her throat.

He grabbed a bath sponge, soaked it and squirted body wash onto it. With a thick lather worked up, he opened a small gap between their bodies and massaged the suds onto Bryce's back. The hot water and relaxing touch of his strong hands guiding the sponge made her sleepy. She sighed, the sound one of pure bliss.

"I thought we'd go by my studio this afternoon," he suggested. "It's off Alameda."

His words pulled Bryce from her reverie and she wasn't sure what bothered her more—the idea of going out in public with him or the fact that he was successful enough to have a separate studio and had directly avoided mentioning it until now. She glanced at Diaz over her shoulder. He was staring at her back, his gaze following his hands as the sponge stroked down her side, along her tailbone and up her other side. Finished with her back, he brought the sponge up to her breasts, moving it in slow circles first around the perimeter of one breast and then the other. He moved in a horizontal eight, the figure drawn tighter and tighter until he was just moving from nipple to nipple.

"A separate studio, a two bedroom apartment without a roommate and Courvoisier," she said, trying to concentrate on something other than the hypnotic dance of the sponge over her rigid nipples. "You're not a really famous painter, are you?"

"Not yet," he answered and let the sponge fall between her relaxed legs.

"Then how do you pay for all this?"

He kept one hand on her chest, teasing a nipple until her entire breast swelled from the delightful torment of his strong and nimble fingertips. Leaning forward, he pressed against her back, forcing her breast into his palm. His other hand reached between her legs where the sponge had disappeared beneath the soapy water.

"If you really want to know," he told her, his fingertips finding the hard line of her clit and beginning to rub, "I'll tell you..." Keeping his thumb moving in maddeningly tight circles, he slid his index and middle finger lower, finding her hot core.

Bryce lifted her bottom from the tub, one hip higher than the other to ease the entry of his fingers. "You'll tell me?" She wanted to know, but right now she really wanted him to fuck her, his fingers a preliminary tease to the thick cock that shifted against her lower back.

She lifted higher and felt the tip of his erection graze the cleavage of her ass. His hand slid beneath her, found the entrance to her cunt and held his cock steady as she slowly settled onto his lap.

When she was halfway down, he gripped both of her hips and controlled her descent. "Yes, I'll tell you..." he said, leaving her body and mind waiting as his swollen head stretched her wide.

Bryce waited for him—to ram into her, to tell her, to do both hard and fast. She bit down, sensing the sharp thrust before he released it.

"I'll tell you Monday."

⊠ ⊠ ⊠

Bryce gave a little whimper of protest but didn't stop moving against Walt. Her pussy was hot and tighter-than-tight despite the heat and soap. He ground his hips and then pressed his palm between her shoulder blades, forcing her to lean forward and expose more of her body to him. She couldn't hide within the tub's confines, though he knew she wanted to. Wrapping the length of her hair around his hand, he forced her further forward until she was on her knees in the tub. Her breasts pressed flat against the white enamel and she gripped the sides for support.

His cock twitched inside her and he withdrew until half his length remained concealed. He unknotted his fist from her hair but kept light pressure against the small of her back with his open palm. With his other hand, he spread her butt cheeks further apart. He had to control her pleasure this time instead of falling mindlessly in after her, lost in her soft moans and yielding flesh.

"Ah, Brycie, you're so hot."

And she was hot, the air around them steaming with her lush, sultry perfection. He watched her pussy hug his uncut cock, his shaft pushing deep and slow into her while the sheath of skin moved only a little. Her ass winked at him and he fished around in the soapy water to find the sponge. He squeezed the water from the sponge over her tail bone, watched it run across the tight pink star and down until it cascaded around his cock. He did it again, and Bryce gripped the sides of the tub harder, flinging her head back and grinding against him.

Walt dropped the sponge into the water and ran the pad of his index finger over the sensitive skin of her nether hole. It contracted beneath his touch, quivering with a nervous anticipation that made the skin covering his balls pull tight with his own excitement. He kept his voice soft and caressing as he increased the pressure he was applying. "Brycie, you said just your mouth was virgin?"

When she only moaned in response, he slowly wiggled the very tip of his finger into the ring of muscles that guarded her ass. She was so incredibly tight there. He couldn't believe she had dared to fuck herself in the ass. But then he'd never met a girl who had taken her own virginity before. The thought of taking her there with his finger, stroking the warm velvet of her ass while he pounded her pussy, made his balls ache harder.

"Bryce," he asked again, his voice not so soft or caressing. "Only your mouth, right?"

"Mmm...yes," she moaned, pussy and ass pulling at him, questing for more. "Take what you want, Walt."

Bryce ended her sentence with a small cry of need and he felt a sense of victory wash over him. Whatever negative ideas she held about her body, she wasn't thinking them now. She was down to how good it felt, how good he was making her feel. And he would bring her back to this point again and again this weekend, taking her sweet mouth and ass and pussy until she would finally let him take *and* keep what he really wanted—her heart.

"Slow down, Brycie," he cautioned, emotion thick in his throat. Cock still, he worked his finger into her ass, watching the tip disappear. Her cunt fluttered around him and she hyperventilated with need. He kept her perched there, tightening his perineum so that his cock moved inside her without him thrusting.

He slid his finger in to the middle joint, gently moving it in a small, dipping circle. She turned her head to the side, her cheek against the cool enamel coating of the tub. Her lips were parted and colored a dark, blood infused cherry. A matching spot of color flushed the apple of her cheek. She was close to coming now, her hips moving to match his pace. He started to stroke both holes, his finger sliding all the way in.

She had every muscle locked around him. Her grinds had turned desperate and short, her body almost in seizure as her second climax overtook her first. His finger worked her ass and she straightened at the waist. She let her weight pull her down so that he pushed deeper into her, great contractions rolling through her as she came again and collapsed forward.

Walt eased from Bryce, settled back in the big tub and pulled her to him. She twisted until she was three-quarters on her stomach, her lower body nestled between his spread legs. She rested against him, their bodies chest-to-chest. He stilled his thoughts, focusing only on the feeling of her lips as they brushed against his collar bone.

He knew she was tired and sated, too content to worry about her body. He also knew it would take a lot more to move her beyond this being a merely transitory state in which she was Bryce the Beautiful—the lush creature that fueled his every fantasy. But, for the moment, his satisfaction was complete.

Chapter Twelve

Dressed once again in the black georgette, the charm bracelet securely around her wrist, Bryce waited while Diaz came around to her side of his parked Suburban and opened the door for her. She stood next to him while he made sure the vehicle's doors were locked, and then they started across the lot to the building that housed his studio.

They were just off E. Alameda Avenue and the sound of passing railcars drowned out any chance of conversation as they walked. The area was at the top end of being low-rent for Glendale, but she still couldn't imagine paying for both an apartment and space in one of the buildings. As she'd learned on the drive over, he was paying for an entire floor.

"I've got some paperwork to take care of while I'm here," Diaz said, inserting and turning a key in the elevator panel. "It should only take me about half an hour, so have a look around and I'll give you the grand tour when I'm finished."

The elevator stopped at the loft level and he slid the gate back, letting Bryce enter first. She didn't need to wait until Monday for Diaz to admit to being a trust fund baby or someone who'd managed to get out of the market before the dot.com craze went dot.bust—this studio said it all. The space was huge, the area directly in front of the elevator furnished with a midnight blue sofa and pearl gray love seat in a short napped velvet. The seating surrounded a large square coffee table made of a light colored wood that looked something like a pickled oak. She wasn't exactly sure what type of wood it was, but knew the table wasn't a garage sale find. The desk he sat down at to take care of his paperwork matched the coffee table and had a cushioned low back chair. Until she reached the actual work area of the studio, she felt like she had walked into a Casa Armani showroom.

The rest of the loft area was all business, though. There were canvases in groupings, not as if they were on display, but warehoused as if to suit the building's original purpose before it had been converted. Some paintings were waiting to be framed and packaged. Others were wrapped in plain brown paper for pickup. These sat next to shipping boxes and crates, as well as the more practical canvas tubes. Bryce discreetly looked at the shipping labels. Most were merely tagged for a courier service without a buyer's name, but she knew all the trendy and star-filled neighborhoods as well as any other Angelino.

Maybe he isn't a trust baby after all, she thought as she bent down to examine the first unwrapped painting. It was a nude of a middle-aged black woman. She was smaller than Bryce, but her body was a sensuous example of her heritage. She was propped against white fur, her dark gleaming skin stretched over full hips and heavy breasts. Her hand rested between plump thighs as if she'd been caught mid-caress.

Forcing her thoughts away from what Diaz must have felt painting women who looked caught in a moment of passion, Bryce bent lower to see if the portrait was dated. She smiled; the mahogany goddess was over a year old and Bryce would have remembered the woman if she'd ever shown up at the apartment building while Bryce was going in or out.

Above the date was his artist mark. She couldn't read it at first, would have sworn it was written in a blocked *kanji*, but then, tilting her head, she saw it was pure tagger techno. Would a trust fund baby sign his name like a graffiti artist, she wondered?

The initials were reversed, the "D" before the "G", with something like a Gemini symbol or a Roman II forming the bridge between the letters. Bryce straightened, wondering whether she should interpret it as "Galtero Diaz the Gemini", or "Galtero Diaz the Second"? And if it was the latter, was Papa Diaz the Napa Valley vintner?

And, oh, dear God, no—that would make Artemesia Diaz his mother?

While it was only through her perverse fetish for the local gossip columns that Bryce had ever heard of the woman, Bryce felt she had every reason to believe

Artemesia Diaz was pure bitch. The idea of having to meet her was terrifying—overriding the reality that things would be over with Diaz come Monday. Artemesia subscribed to the existence of two types of women—those who were served and those who serve. Absent the right pedigree from birth, you could never be more than a servant. And it was a well-known fact that every up-and-comer in Hollywood had better be prepared to kiss her well-toned ass if they wanted to join any foundation or club she held a board directorship on.

More like a board dictatorship, she thought and turned to where Diaz was supposed to be doing paperwork but sat watching her instead.

"You don't like it?" he asked, misreading the look of horror on her face.

Bryce looked over her shoulder at the picture he had nodded at—the untitled mahogany goddess. "She's beautiful," Bryce said. "You painted her beautifully."

She chewed on the inside of her cheek for a few seconds and toed the concrete flooring with her shoe. "Uhm...when were you born?"

"Tax Day," he smiled. "Nineteen seventy-two."

April fifteenth, she didn't know whether that was Gemini or not. "And what sign would that be?"

"Sign?"

She could almost hear the laughter in his voice. She nodded.

"Aren't you supposed to use that question to get me into bed?"

Bryce frowned at him and mustered up her most commanding voice. "Just answer the question, Diaz," she said. "Or I'll be forced to leave and find a paper or something to figure it out on my own."

"Aries." Blurted, like a child about to lose a favorite toy.

Is he sure? she wondered and asked, "Not Gemini?"

He shook his head, his mouth somewhere between a frown and a bemused grin. "You're not going to say we're star-crossed now—ill fated and all that?"

"No," she answered and waved him back to his paperwork before moving to the next picture. If there was going to be any silver lining to Monday's dark clouds, not having to be introduced to Artemesia Diaz as her son's new girlfriend was definitely it.

"Where do your parents live?" she asked, taking a different tack.

"Oh, uhm," he began, his attention seeming to re-focus on the paperwork with a jerk. "Dad's, uh, well, kinda off in his own little kingdom and Mother is local."

Dad versus Mother? Little kingdom? She dissected his choice of words, looking for clues both on the identity of his parents and his relationship with them. Something, she felt, was definitely going on in his use of "Mother" with a capital "M". As for "little kingdom"—Artemesia, of course, only left L.A. for Europe and Galtero Senior seldom left his vineyards. With more land than some small European countries, it would definitely qualify as a private kingdom. "Are they divorced?"

"Ah...just kinda *separate*, really."

Bryce offered a sympathetic "I see", and turned to look at the next painting.

"This isn't going to work."

Heart stilling, Bryce turned to find him stuffing the paperwork back into a desk drawer. He stood and started across the room, a devious smile on his face as he watched her. But she wasn't the prey he was stalking, at least not yet. He was headed for a cabinet that, given the rainbow assortment of splashed paint on it, probably held supplies.

"What's not going to work?" she asked.

"Trying to do invoices when I could be doing you."

His answer should have seemed crass, instead it made her instantly wet, particularly when he was smiling at her like that. "And you're going into a supply closet, why?"

He was opening boxes, grabbing and discarding handfuls of charcoal and pastels before moving on to the next container. "Body markers," he answered. "I know I have them here somewhere from last Halloween—I figure if I can't have you long enough for me to paint you in the flesh, you'll let me paint your flesh."

Finding the box of markers, he tucked them in the waistband of his pants and took his hunt to the footlockers stacked next to the supply cabinet. From the top trunk, he pulled a blood-red faux fur and spread it on the floor. Sinking onto his knees in the plush pile, he reeled his ultimate prey in with a tilt of his head and the play of his hands down the front of his shirt as he undressed.

Bryce came to him, stopping at the edge of the carpet to step from her sandals. She was intent on disrobing in the same unrevealing manner she had used at the apartment, but Diaz held something else in mind.

"No. You're going to let me undress you."

He grabbed her hips, and the sudden action forced her to place her hand on his shoulder or risk falling. Even after she felt steady, she kept her hand there, her attention absorbed by the way the sunlight in the room gave his skin a golden glow.

"Starting with this," he said, and reached for the charm bracelet.

Bryce had to wonder if he had some sort of reverse psychic ability—his intuition taking him straight to the one thing it was essential she leave on. "It won't get damaged," she said, failing to hide her hand before he could catch her by the wrist.

"No, but it gets caught in my hair." He looked up at her, his smile disingenuous as he gave the dark locks a shake.

Oh, he was so lying to her. "You've never mentioned it before."

"And you've never mentioned why you're so attached to it," he said before casually dropping the suggestion, "Was it a gift from some almost lover?"

Even with the short amount of time they'd spent together, Bryce knew he was only feigning disinterest. She let the shock show on her face. *He was jealous? Actually jealous?*

"My maiden aunt," she answered and plucked at the hem of her shirt. "You remember?"

He pocketed the bracelet and then grabbed the waistband of her pants. With his other hand, he held hers, his head bowed, lips hovering over it. "If I lose it, I will beg her forgiveness on my knees." He finished the vow with a kiss.

"And what about my forgiveness," she teased, bringing her hand up to play in the rich silk of his hair.

"Oh, Brycie baby," he said and started the slow removal of her pants, "you've already got me down on my knees."

▨ ▨ ▨

And the things he was going to do to her.

Walt pulled Bryce's pants and underwear down together, stopping when the full split of her labia came into view. The loft was kept cool only by high placed fans and a light sheen of moisture covered her bald mound. A thicker syrup glistened at the seam of her pussy. He pressed his lips to her mound, his tongue flicking out to taste her earthy flavor. Pulling Bryce's clothes lower, he broke the seal of flesh and honey with his tongue and stroked her clit.

She had both hands tangled in his hair now, her thighs and ass trembling with the anticipation of his sucking and licking her to climax. He took a few more leisurely swipes at the line of her pussy, lowering his body and tilting his head up so that he could probe her cunt with each lick.

Every time he touched Bryce, she was slicker than the time before, her apparent desire for him never waning. It made him hotter, more desperate to be in her, to have her beyond a short fling. He wanted to know just how wet he could make her. It seemed as if he'd only just scratched the surface. The promise of an even wilder, more passionate lover lurked beneath her shy, self-conscious reserve.

Impatient to mark her as his, Walt pulled the pants the rest of the way down and helped her kick them to the side. Then he ordered her down on her knees. When he had the shirt up over her head, her arms still inside and raised high, he had to fight off the impulse to use the shirt as an impromptu binding.

But he had the markers for that, he reminded himself. He stripped the rest of the shirt away and pressed Bryce down onto the fur. She looked up at him, then looked away in a half-coy gesture. He placed the box of markers next to her and stood to remove the rest of his clothing. Stepping from his shoes, he could see that she was fighting the need to cover herself.

"No, Bryce," he warned. Barefoot now, he used his foot to coax her legs further apart, so that her lips opened and he could see the full, dew dropped flower of her sex. He pushed his pants over his hips and his erection popped into view.

"Let me see you touching yourself, Brycie," he ordered, his voice thick as his cock and jumping with the same need. She hesitated, and he hardened his command. "Just rest your finger against it."

She wanted to, he felt that. Fresh cream dampened her pussy at the rough slide of his voice and, when she finally obeyed, she instantly jerked and moaned. Forgetting her embarrassment, she stroked the tip of her finger the length of her clit, stopping at its end to pinch and roll the engorged hood. She moaned, then bit her bottom lip.

Was she trying, he wondered, *to silence any other traitorous sound?*

It didn't matter. Bryce belonged to him at that moment, no matter what she might say or do later. She was his to command or worship. She could bite that pretty little lip all she wanted. There was nothing she could do to hide the intense need charging the air around them like an electrical storm.

Fully undressed, he sank to his knees and pulled a red body marker from the box. Pushing her knees apart, Walt lay between her legs and kissed the inside fold of her left thigh. And since she was swollen and creaming just for him, he uncapped the red marker and put his artist's mark in the spot he had just kissed.

Bryce glanced at her leg just long enough to acknowledge his subtle claiming before she pushed her shoulders and head against the floor. The motion caused a slight lift of her bottom, raising the puffed lips of her cunt to demand his kiss. He kissed her, lightly, and then gently took one of her swollen labia between his teeth. Softly, he pulled. Holding the marker in his right hand, he threaded his arm under her left leg and back over her hip. Holding her steady, he continued his careful teething and drew a pentacle enclosed in a pentagon to the side of her abdomen, just past the soft bump of her hip. His Venus, hot and sensual, ripe and so very fuckable. When the mark was made, he took her clit into his mouth, his tender suckling pushing her another inch closer to oblivion.

With her body telling him she was a breath away from climaxing, he withdrew his pressure, bypassing her mound on his way up to kiss her navel. Beneath the dip of her belly button, he drew a two-horned crown, its center filled with an enormous pearl. Reaching her firm and ready breasts, he drew a circle with an inverted cross at the bottom of the left breast. *This is for the daughter she will bear me.*

He took her nipple in his mouth, his pressure bruising a fresh blush of passion from her as his free hand reached between Bryce's legs to stroke more heat into her pussy. When he brought her to the brink of climax once more, he stopped. Only the marker touched her as he drew a circle with an arrow shooting out its side on her right breast. *And this is for the son she will bear me.*

He began licking and kissing the breast, his hand keeping it gripped firmly in place. With his lower torso, he kept her thighs spread, his weight pressing her legs open in a wanton's position. Pulling three fingers into a tight triangle, he invaded her pussy and stroked her hard while he sucked and squeezed at her breast.

Bryce was panting, squirming against the fur's crimson mat. When she was just at the point of screaming his name and filling his hand with her slick honey, he pulled back again.

She did scream his name, her voice drenched in frustration. But mercy and relief would have to come later. He placed the tip of the marker just left of center on her breast bone and drew his artist's mark once again. It didn't matter to him that the ink would last only a week or so. He willed that she would always see it.

"Please, Walt."

She was pleading for him now, her agile hands pinching and squeezing the succulent breasts that would one day nourish his children. The thought brought his cock to a new level of hardness and he moved down to leave one last mark before he relented to their mutual need. Over her mound, another circle, the line leaving it stopping at the top of her labial split. He drew the line of Venus's cross, and then, at the split, the hard "V" of Mars's manhood.

Walt replaced the marker and pushed the box off the fur blanket. Fisting his cock, he teased her pussy, making sure she was ready to take him. Her faint, rhythmic moans had him so hard and swollen that he was afraid of hurting her. Her cunt looked like it was all cream and honey, but he could feel how tight she was, and he wasn't sure he would be able to fit inside her completely this time.

Leaning low over Bryce's body, Walt positioned the head of his cock at the center of her opening. She was pushing against and around his cock head, trying to pull him in before he started another round of teasing.

"Slow, Brycie," he cautioned. If her pussy didn't stop sucking at his dick, he was going to anoint the marks he'd made on her clear, supple skin. The thought alone of coming on her stomach and creamy thighs made his cock twitch and he had to squeeze the base hard.

"Roll over." He couldn't see her like this—her whole body begging to be fucked—and keep control.

Bryce rolled over, lifting the drenched rosebud of her cunt up in offering. Walt put his palm on the small of her back, forcing her stomach and hips back onto the fur. Wedging Bryce's legs open with his thighs, he entered her pussy in one fast, slick thrust. When he was embedded inside her, he let the full weight of his torso rest on her back. He pushed her arms away from her body, snaking his own under her armpits and then gripping her shoulders from beneath.

Locked tight to Bryce, her body immobilized, Walt began to gently roll his hips. The sensation was delicious. Her pussy was incredibly hot, her desire making her just slick enough so that he could move while she clamped down on him. With every little stroke Walt made, Bryce punctuated it with a sharp pant.

"Are you coming for me, Brycie?" he asked. "Can you feel it building, taking everything away but just you and me?"

"Yes!"

Delirious, Bryce's whole body was an inferno, the flames licking at his skin and threatening to singe his hair.

"You don't want me to stop?" He didn't stop, he kept grinding inside her pussy, each thrust and hip roll crushing more of her resistance to powder.

"No, please don't."

"You don't want me to stop now."

"No, I said 'no'."

"And tomorrow, is this sweet body mine?"

"Yes, please—" The pre-orgasmic tremor that ran through her body cut off the rest of her plea.

He made his thrusts tighter, more powerful, his cock swelling from his own looming climax.

"And the day after that," he pushed. "You *do* want to be with me the day after that, don't you, Brycie?"

Everything was shutting down to short, intense twitches and gripping contractions. When he thought he couldn't swell any thicker, that her cunt couldn't hold him any tighter, the pressure built higher until he almost didn't hear her answer.

"Yes!" she screamed, her control disintegrating in the explosion of her climax. "The day after that—I want you every day, Walt Diaz."

Chapter Thirteen

Sitting in the passenger seat of Walt's Suburban, Bryce fiddled with the charm bracelet. *Yeah, so what?* she thought. She had finally admitted the truth. Did he have to gloat about it?

Apparently, he did.

She twisted in her seat, trying not to make eye contact with him. At least he wasn't gloating out loud— not yet, anyway. *I want you every day, Walt Diaz!* How fucking corny was that? Her, being all schmaltzy over a man. Okay, a sweet man, intelligent, caring and sensitive. A man whose tremendously large cock came with its own slide belt. Still, *I want you every day?* That had to come from Erato's book of phrases because it sure as hell didn't come from her own.

Walt finally broke the silence. "Do you want dinner in, or out?"

Bryce gave a definitive "In". It had been hard enough when they'd stopped for gas and the women had visibly ogled Walt as he lounged against the Suburban's side. And then their gazes had invariably skipped up to the front of the vehicle to see what lucky girl was in the passenger seat. For the most part, it was only the strength of the reactions that were mixed, from the curled lip and mouthed "what the fuck?" to the politely arched, but incredulous brow. Only one woman had given Bryce a thumbs up accompanied by a silent "woot" of approval.

An hour or more of sitting in a restaurant, people watching them, watching her eat, glossing over their own imperfections as they smugly counted Bryce's calories for her—well, she wouldn't exactly wilt, but it wasn't the best use of her remaining time with him.

He had his cell phone with him and he pulled it out. "Chinese?"

"Uhm, maybe Korean?"

"Korean it is," he said, dialing from touch and memory while he drove. Once the last number was punched in, he handed the phone to Bryce to place the order.

With at least another half hour's wait for the food once they were back at his apartment, they settled in on the couch. She was exhausted—emotionally and physically. When Walt wrapped his arms around her and just held her, she felt a quiet exaltation. She slipped one arm behind his back and rested the other across his lap. She'd never snuggled before, and it was far from overrated.

Once the food arrived and she picked self-consciously at it, Walt decided to feed her. But even that was nice. The way he followed up each small bite taken with a kiss or a stroke made her stop worrying about her body. Bryce was amazed they weren't naked and rolling on the floor by the time dinner was done. But they weren't. And after he cleared the containers away, he put music on and returned with a sweet wine to chase away the burn of the spicy Korean food.

Stroking Bryce's hair, he sipped his wine, occasionally humming part of the song. His voice was a rich baritone, its undertones vibrating with a tangible sensuality. She put her glass down and rubbed at her eyes. She wanted to curl up in a tight ball on his lap so that he could keep stroking her while he enjoyed the music and his wine. "I think I need a nap."

"A nap sounds perfect," he agreed.

Standing, he took Bryce by the hand and led her into the bedroom. Despite her groggy protests that she could do it herself and that it wasn't necessary, he undressed her. His hands lingered momentarily on the symbols he had covered her body with. He pressed his fingertips to his mouth, just once, as if remembering the taste of her body, and then he covered her with a light satin quilt. When she was tucked in, he bent down and kissed her, his hand stroking her honey-blonde hair until she closed her eyes and fell asleep.

▨ ▨ ▨

Bryce slept through until early morning. She woke to find Walt curled up next to her and the air conditioner going full blast. She eased up onto an elbow and saw that he had left a robe hanging on each of the bed's end posts. The kimono she had worn Friday night was on his side and a dark russet satin robe hung from her post. She eased from the bed and slipped the robe on. It was roomy, with a soft brushed cotton lining. The thought that Erato had left it hanging on the post tempted Bryce, but the hem touched the floor and she could smell traces of the warm, masculine scents she had come to associate with Walt.

Knowing she could spend the morning watching him sleep, Bryce didn't risk a backwards glance as she left the bedroom. At the bathroom door, she hesitated, her muscles tensing in anticipation of finding that Erato had popped back in. She opened the door and flipped the light on. No muse, just the travel kit.

No new clothes, either.

Hanging the robe on the door hook, Bryce sighed. Cinderella only received one dress—it was time to pull out the credit cards if she wanted to keep seeing Walt's eyes pop the way they had with the two outfits Erato had given her already. Turning the shower on, she ran a hand over one breast and firmly thumbed its nipple. His eyes didn't pop when she was naked. They grew all smoky and intense. Just thinking about the way he looked at her during those moments made her hot.

She reached over, turned the warm water down and grabbed the body wash. She smiled, careful not to let her hands linger too long on any one body part. There was no point in wasting the caresses when there was a perfectly gorgeous male naked in bed and ready to fulfill her fantasies. Still, she couldn't help but pause and trace the signs he'd drawn on her with the body markers. He'd done it in an almost cabalistic manner, the symbols and sex working together to create an invisible bond to hold them together beyond the weekend.

Why not? she thought as she left the shower and dried off. If Erato could perform magic, why couldn't she and Walt have worked some of their own?

Her hands touched the two artist's marks he'd left on her, one at the heart, one in the crease of her thigh. The memory rose up in perfect detail—his body gloriously naked and cock-proud, his expression tender yet filled with dark sorceries. He'd meant to do it, too, she realized. In some superstitious, subconscious way, he was giving the universe warning that she was his and his alone.

Hands still touching his marks, Bryce felt twin contractions. Heart and womb were telling her it was time to wake the man that had mastered them.

Upon leaving the bathroom, she found that the gorgeous male in question was no longer naked or in bed. He was one the living room floor, the kimono loose around him as he stretched.

"I was going to wake you." She could feel a pout pushing her lips out, and she folded her hands behind her back. The urge to put them on her hips and give her foot a little stamp worthy of a two-year-old was strong. But then he smiled and something warm and fuzzy replaced her petulance.

She went to the couch and positioned herself so that she could watch him do his stretching exercises. Underneath the robe, he was wearing semi-loose cotton boxer briefs. She had left him naked in bed and she wasn't sure she liked the change. She giggled and instantly clapped a hand over her mouth. His gorgeous uncut cock probably would look silly in all those stretching positions. At least, if it were soft.

At the moment, he was doing a butterfly stretch, sitting with his knees out and his heels pulled close to his bottom. Every few seconds, he bent at the waist and held the position.

Bryce glanced at his lap. She could feel a slow blush creep across her cheeks. The fabric had a perceptible bulge. He wasn't soft. Nor was he hard—not yet.

"Stop that." His voice was quiet and held the barest tinge of embarrassment.

"Stop what?" She tried to make her question sound innocent, as if she wasn't staring at his cock and willing it to grow bigger and bolder.

"Looking at me...*there*." His protest ended with a little groan. "It's having an effect."

"My looking at it?" Less innocence, more of a pleased squeal. It *was* having an effect. He was growing harder by the second.

"Yes."

Ah, he sounded almost desperate now. She could practically hear him thinking what he wanted to do with her, what would be a proper punishment for her being deliberately naughty and getting him all hard like that. She giggled again, brought both hands up to her mouth and rolled onto her back, eyes closed.

When she was sure the giggles were gone, she slowly removed her hands. She glanced in the direction of his lap, her neck straining to keep the cock check as discreet as possible. Rock hard. She smiled and somehow managed an exaggerated sigh.

"You do need to stretch," she admitted. "And get a workout in—you lift weights every day, don't you?" She didn't need to ask, she listened to it every day. Monday, Wednesday, Friday and Saturday were heavy workouts— lots of weights, lots of repetitions. The other three days were light.

"Every day," he agreed.

"And you didn't get to yesterday," she pointed out. "And it's making you...uhm...*stiff.*"

Walt growled at her, pushed onto his knees and crawled slowly to the couch. He nipped her ear before tracing the curve of her jaw. "You know what's making me stiff, minx."

Biting her lip, she resisted the impulse to invite him up onto the couch. "Finish your stretches," she ordered.

"They're done."

His hand crept under her robe and she grabbed his wrist. "Well, if you're done with your stretches, you should shower and then work out."

An intense lust pulled at his features and she had to close her eyes or give in immediately. Only, closing her eyes filled her mind with images of Walt on the weight bench while she straddled his thick cock.

"You want to watch me work out." Not a question. He knew.

"Yes," she answered in a whisper.

Breaking her light hold on his wrist, he slid his hand down to where her legs were pressed tightly together. His lips caressed her ear as he teased her pussy. "I think you're already watching me work out."

He ran his nails lightly over her mons, raising the trace of hair that had already grown back. He brushed his own morning stubble against her cheek, kissing her on the mouth as her thighs started to flutter from the tension of keeping him out.

"A quick shower."

She nodded, trembling.

"A long work out."

She licked her lips, nodded again.

Only when she heard the bathroom door shut and the shower turn on did Bryce dare open her eyes. She got up and dragged the leather ottoman until it was against the side of the couch in a spot where she could sit facing him while he lifted weights at the bench.

She had just finished positioning the ottoman when the water cut off. She sat down, one arm curling over the couch's overstuffed arm. Resting her cheek on her hand, she waited for the bathroom door to open. Walt didn't make her wait long. He exited the bathroom two minutes later, the robe's sash loosely tied around his waist so that the kimono was only partially closed. His hair was still wet and slicked back.

Grinning at her, he straddled the weight bench. He grabbed the sash's simple knot, his gaze playing over the robe she was wearing. He sucked his bottom lip in, the arch of his brow suggesting to Bryce a quid pro quo.

She undid her sash and pulled at the edges of the robe until her shoulders and the top swell of her breasts were exposed. Walt's sash came off and his erection pressed forward to push the robe open. Bryce's mouth opened in an appreciative "O". He ran his fingertips down the length of his cock and back up to smooth the foreskin away from the succulent red tip.

Bryce smoothed her fingers along the edge of the robe until they were even with her cunt. She bent her leg, planting a foot flat on the ottoman. The fold of the robe slid behind her, exposing her pussy as she dipped her fingers into its heat. She ran her other hand through her still damp hair, arching, her excited moan unfaked.

Walt stripped away the rest of his robe and lay back on the weight bench. Spacing his hands about a foot apart, he gripped the weight bar. He had some eighty pounds stacked on the bar and the bar itself weighed another forty-five pounds. He lifted and brought the bar down to about an inch above his chest. He extended his arms, bringing the weights back up and then repeated the press. She watched the way the different parts of his body worked together to lift the weights. The chest and arms had the heaviest job, but she could see the rippled muscles of his abs tense, and the pull on his ass and thighs made his erect cock bob on each upward push of the bar.

At twenty, he stopped and returned the bar to its holder. He rose up and twisted until his upper body weight rested on one arm and he could watch Bryce. The muscles on his chest had swelled slightly from the workout, the veins on his biceps standing out in light relief.

He dropped his gaze to where her hand still rested against her thigh. "Twenty strokes, Brycie."

She brought her other foot up and shifted on the ottoman until both feet were pointed in his direction. She still wore the robe, but it fell loosely around her, the front of her body exposed to him. Spreading her legs, Bryce leaned against the arm of the couch and splayed her pussy lips with the inverted "V" of her index and middle finger. She slid her middle finger to center, her ring finger keeping her lips separated as she took her first long stroke. She started at the wet mouth of her cunt, slicking the juices up over her clit. When she finished the return downward stroke, she heard Walt count it off, his voice tightly reined in.

"One, Brycie."

She whimpered as she started the next stroke. Nineteen more and she would be coming in front of him. She finished the stroke and quickly started the next so that he was counting off the third almost before he finished the second.

The heat in his voice stroked her skin as she masturbated for him. She couldn't keep the rest of her body still. She flexed her hips and wiggled her ass as the numbers got bigger and she came closer to the sharp edge of orgasm.

"Twenty, Brycie."

Fingers lingering in the moist pocket of her cunt, she didn't need to look at Walt to know he was wearing a wicked smile—she knew it from the way he shaped the words, how he said her name. When she did look at him, she felt a wave of heat and sexual tension roll over her body. From his expression, she knew he didn't want her to stop. But it was equally clear he wanted to keep playing this little game he'd started.

Getting off the bench, he took the bar down. His effort in removing the bar provided Bryce another opportunity to ogle him, the muscles of his back, ass and thighs working together for her erotic entertainment. When the bar and its weights were safely on the floor, he loaded forty pounds onto the leg press and then laid down stomach first on the bench. Even though the position should have accommodated his erection, he stuck his arms beneath him. Palms and forearms flat against the bench, he tensed his thighs and butt and raised his cock off the cushioned surface. The edge of the bench pressed into the front of his thighs as he positioned his Achilles tendons against the underside of the leg press handles. Locked everywhere but at the knees, he pumped out twenty leg presses. As he moved, her gaze darted over his body. The bob of his cock with each press had her pussy twitching. And the way his ass tensed—well, it made her want to jump up and bite into one firm cheek. It was over all too soon.

Reps finished, Walt stood up and approached the ottoman, his hips swaying like a gunslinger's as he crossed the short distance. She smiled. He was definitely packing steel. And heat. When he stopped in front of her, she sat up and nuzzled his erection. There was a light sheen of perspiration below the cut of his abs and she licked at it, the salt making her eager to have his cock in her mouth and the taste of his cum on her tongue.

Taking his cock in one hand, she smoothed the foreskin down and sucked at the tip. Walt moaned with pleasure, but put his hands on her shoulders and gently pushed her away from his cock.

"Your turn, Bryce. Twenty."

She started to roll onto her stomach. He stopped her with another light touch to her shoulder.

"On the bench, Brycie."

🔯🔯🔯

Walt looked down to where Bryce lay on the bench. She was stomach down, her back and lush bottom presented to him from the way the back of her feet held the leg press bar. He had removed twenty pounds, leaving enough weight that she could make smooth presses without injuring her muscles.

She was looking to one side, her right cheek resting on the back of her hands. He knelt on the side of the bench she faced. His left hand pressed gently between her shoulder blades, while the other rested on her bottom.

"First lift doesn't count," he warned. He moved his right hand down to cup her shin. "First is for form, 'kay?"

Bryce nodded and when Walt increased the pressure against her shin, she drew the weights up, then slowly let them back down as his touch lightened.

"Good." He slid both hands along her body, his left moving down to the small of her back while his right traveled up to where her thighs gated her pussy. Slowly he worked his middle and ring fingers into the slick well of her cunt. She squeezed around him and his cock reacted with a jealous throb.

"Lift."

She made the first press slow and tentative, and he probed her pussy in the same manner. The second lift he had to tell her to slow down. His body protested the command. He wanted to finger fuck her to a hard, fast screaming climax and then bury his cock in her tight little cunt before the contractions could subside.

On her fifth lift, there was a deep tremble of sound at the back of her throat and he groaned. It was the second time she'd whimpered this afternoon, the sound one of complete submission to his sexual will. He wanted to possess her now. He dipped his head until his lips rested lightly against one soft butt cheek. He draped his left bicep across the small of her back, his forearm pressed against her right hip as he hugged her to him. He pressed his lips around the yielding flesh for a second, allowing himself a pseudo bite to keep from consuming her whole. If she whimpered again, there was no way he could manage a slow conquering of her pussy.

"Lift." He growled the order, thrusting a third finger into her cunt. The growl kept rumbling through his throat until his lips were trembling against her bottom in a rough purr, and she obeyed.

She lifted again, without his order, finding a rhythm that kept her pushing towards the first wave of her approaching climax.

Walt's hand unwrapped from around her hip and he reached up, tangling his fingers in the honey-blonde hair and forcing her to arch her neck. She had finished her twentieth press but he was still stroking her cunt, his fingers pistoning inside her.

"Come for me, Brycie." His voice bordered on sexual desperation but never quite crossed over. "Come for me, baby, so I can fuck this sweet hole."

Bryce brought the weights up one last time and held them there. Her cunt was locked down, gripping Walt's fingers in place as the muscles rolled over them in a milking motion. Her chest was off the weight bench, her arms supporting her as she panted out her climax.

Legs trembling, she slowly returned the leg press to its resting position. Walt released her hair and she lowered her chest back down to the bench. Her eyelids fluttered from the strength of her climax and her lips trembled as she drew in short breaths.

Withdrawing from her, Walt planted a kiss on her shoulder. "Stay there, Brycie, I'll be right back."

He went into the bathroom, returning a few seconds later with a small tub of massage cream. He scooped some into his palm, warming it before he began massaging her tight shoulder and back muscles. When he was done with her back, he ordered her into a sitting position and sat facing her on the bench. He placed the tub of cream on the bench between them and then rubbed the front of her shoulders.

Bryce dipped into the tub and started rubbing his thighs and hips, arching into Walt's hands as he massaged her breasts. She nuzzled his neck, her question hot against the sensitive skin of his throat.

"I thought you wanted to fuck me?"

He was rubbing her nipples, his thumbs running along the insides in tight circles. He groaned, took more cream and kneaded her thighs. "I do."

Bryce pressed one palm against his chest, pushing him back as she set the tub on the floor. "Will it hold...us?" she asked as she stood and straddled his body over the bench.

He nodded as his hands roamed her thighs and ass. "It'll hold four of us."

Bryce reached down and squeezed his erection before she guided his cock into her. Her cunt was slick from her climax, but his cock was swollen, full and throbbing with the need for release. She drew him in slowly, letting her weight push her down until her bottom pressed lightly against the front of his thighs and he was completely in her. She bent to the side to gather more massage cream and he flexed inside her.

God, not that sexy little whimper again. Walt grabbed her hips and held her tight to him as she massaged the cream onto his chest and abdomen. She pushed down as she massaged his stomach, riding him tighter the harder she pressed.

He could see the sensation building in her. Her lips parted and she began to pant. Her features contorted as if her concentration focused solely on the contours of his cock as he rotated his hips beneath her. She relaxed her knees and her weight settled more solidly against his body. She tossed her head back and placed both palms flat against his chest, gripping him with muscles he'd never discovered in any of his other lovers. He was deep inside her now, hitting against the opening to her cervix, and she moaned.

"Oh!"

Her exclamation was almost a scream and she followed it quickly with another. He watched Bryce as she turned into a wild creature. Her weight kept their bodies cinched together. The plump folds of her labia molded to his lower abdominal muscles with the lips pressed tight together. The intermittent jerks of her upper body had him imagining her clit, hard and sliding between the lips as she rode him. Each little jerk produced a sharp bounce of her firm breasts, pulling his gaze upwards to the cherry-colored tease of her erect nipples.

"Oh, Walt!" She was crying now, hyperventilating as gravity locked her tight around his cock. "I can feel all of you...feel you in me. It's so...so much."

Her eyelids fluttered and Walt strained, waiting for the wave to break and the first moment of rapture to wash over her. When she came, she came with a scream, her hands jumping up to grip his shoulders and pull him in with her.

Chapter Fourteen

They took the caressing and lovers' talk into the bedroom, where the touching escalated and the sheets knotted around their hot sweaty bodies. They drifted to sleep in one another's embrace and didn't wake until four in the evening. In bed, still holding one another, they giggled over the way their stomachs growled from a weekend of neglect.

"We're going out tonight," Walt said, nibbling at Bryce's ear. "That way, I know we won't get distracted and abandon the food."

She frowned, mentally sorting through the contents of her closet and its lack of dinner date clothing. "I can make us something," she said. "And keep my hands off you."

Walt rolled on top of her. "Are you trying to break my heart, Brycie Schoene? Besides, I make no such promise."

When she still hesitated, he stroked her cheek. "And there's someone I want you to meet. He runs the best Baja restaurant in L.A. We need to eat if we're going to knot the sheets up all over again." He finished with a wink that promised another night of complete passion.

"What's the attire?"

Walt laughed. "You put on a tux and I'll wear my Daisy Dukes," he joked. "It won't matter to Victor or anyone else in his restaurant."

"Well, I think I can manage something more appropriate than either," she said and gently pushed on his chest until he let her up. He had folded the outfit she wore on Saturday into a neat pile and she slipped into the clothes, not realizing until she turned back to the bed and saw the soft smile he wore that she'd changed in front of him.

Keeping her expression neutral, she hooked a thumb over her shoulder. "I'll shower and change at home—how long do I have?"

He looked at the clock and then arched a brow. "Forty-five minutes?"

Bryce nodded, studying his face as she agreed to the time limit. She realized she'd been wrong when she'd thought she had memorized his features. All those months of seeing him on her way in or out, she had never dared to look long enough. Now that she could watch him at will, she saw little things she had never noticed before. The silky black brow he'd arched as he teased her had a small scar dipping into it. The scar mixed with his expression to create an almost devilish look, as if he'd been dehorned and that little slice of white was the only thing left to warn her.

That and his smile.

"Forty-three minutes," he said, and his smile widened to a grin.

"Okay, okay." She quick-stepped from the room, ducked into the bathroom to grab the travel kit, and then snatched her keys from the hook by the front door.

She shut Walt's door, pirouetted to her own and unlocked it. Inside her apartment, she headed for her closet, determined to pull something from it that was neither jeans nor a sweatshirt.

"Don't worry about it, dear."

Bryce spun around to find Erato standing in the space she had just walked through. "Oh. You."

Erato put an indignant hand on her hip. "'*Oh. You?*'. What kind of greeting is that?"

"It's just that...that I'd almost forgotten about..." Bryce shrugged and looked down at the bracelet. "You know?"

"That's human grati—" Erato started and then put her arms around Bryce's shoulders. "There, dear. What's the matter?"

"I'd just forgotten." Bryce shrugged away the comfort Erato offered and scratched at her wrist. The dove charm fluttered in response. "About this."

"And you should continue forgetting about it," Erato said, her voice a soft chide. "You've a dinner date to get ready for and less than thirty-nine minutes to do it in."

Bryce shook her head, then wiped away a lone tear. "I just thought that, maybe Monday...maybe he would still..."

"Monday, you're on your own, dear." Erato cupped Bryce's elbow, the touch gentle but unyielding. "Tonight, I'm getting you ready."

Erato steered Bryce toward the bathroom, the water to the shower turning on before the door was even opened. "You've got ten minutes for your shower, no more, and don't worry about getting your hair wet."

Bryce moved into the bathroom, her senses numbed. Twice now, Walt had taken the bracelet away, once in his bathroom and once at the loft. Both times, she'd felt like he'd been looking at her—seeing her exactly as she was and finding her beautiful anyway. Now, with Erato on the other side of the door, telling her to speed it up, Bryce's doubts came flooding back in.

Erato pounded on the door. "Okay, that's enough. Grab a towel because I'm coming in!"

Bryce pulled a towel from the rod and wrapped it around her a second before Erato swept across the bathroom's threshold.

"Leave you alone for a few minutes and your head starts filling with stupid thoughts!"

There was a genuine look of disapproval on the muse's face and Bryce dropped her gaze. *Stupid for thinking it had been just her and Walt in the loft creating their own magic?*

"Bryce Schoene, enough!" Erato herded Bryce in front of the mirror, gathered up the honey-blonde hair that fell halfway down her back and ran a brush through it. On the first swipe, the hair was dry and smooth.

"Open your hand," the muse commanded.

Bryce held her left hand up and opened it.

"No, not that one, the other."

Feeling something thick in her fist, Bryce unclenched her right hand to find a dozen hairpins. Erato took two pins and Bryce could feel the woman twisting and looping the hair, but when she looked in the mirror, she could see little more than a blur of soft gold light.

"I can't see it," she said, and twisted her head to the side.

"You'll see it when I want you to."

"But—"

"Fifteen minutes and we still have makeup and clothes to do," Erato warned.

Bryce started to think there was something quite wrong with the attention Erato was giving her. The thought was interrupted by a pinch at her thigh and the poke of a hairpin against her scalp.

"Ow!" Bryce jerked and then looked down at the blur her legs had become. But what she couldn't see, she could still feel and she didn't like what she was feeling. "Not a garter, nope. Naked, okay, a garter belt, no!"

Erato ignored the complaint, her laugh a soft purr as she pushed past Bryce and sat between the countertop's two sinks. The muse forced her to keep still as she applied a smooth foundation to Bryce's face. Motionless and blocked by Erato's wide shoulders, she couldn't see anything in the mirror. She gave a resigned sigh. Makeup brushes started flashing in and out of the woman's hands. Finally, Erato finished and leaned back against the mirror with a satisfied smile.

She pointed down at Bryce's feet. "Shoes."

Bryce followed the direction of Erato's hand, seeing a glob of gray but knowing from the sudden imbalance that the muse had stuck her in a pair of high-heeled pumps.

"Bag." Erato thrust another gray blur at her.

"I don't like this—not being able to see. I could be dressed like a clown, for all I know."

"What kind of selfish muse are you?" Erato asked.

Seeing Erato's sly expression, Bryce waggled a finger under the goddess's nose. "How does my not being able to see have an effect on Walt's inspiration? What are you hiding?"

"Temps! They have to have everything explained to them and then they're gone two days later." Throwing up her hands, Erato moved so she wasn't blocking the mirror.

Even her face was fuzzy, and Bryce felt the same nausea the toga had invoked rise up.

"Oh, it's not like the toga at all," Erato snapped. Grabbing Bryce by the shoulders, she tilted her head and studied her handiwork. "You feel vulnerable, yes?"

"Yes." Bryce bit the word out.

"And it shows." She smiled, the expression filled with an almost motherly indulgence. "That contradiction—the independent Bryce, the vulnerable Brycie—he loves it and it'll make a wonderful painting."

Bryce felt her stomach settle as Erato offered the explanation.

"Trust me?" the muse asked.

Bryce shook her head. *No.*

"Ha…but you're going anyway, right?"

A nod. *Yes.*

"Good!" Erato's hand swept down toward the knot of fabric nestled in Bryce's shallow cleavage. "Now, about that towel…"

🎨🎨🎨

Returning to Walt's apartment, Bryce opened the door without knocking. She didn't have time to look around the room before a cold, feminine voice assaulted her.

"Must be more than just a casual acquaintance to enter unannounced."

The woman sat on the couch, looking like a Nancy Reagan stick figure but without the horrid red dress. Recognizing Artemesia Diaz from pictures in the society pages, Bryce flinched before she pasted a welcoming smile on her face. When Artemesia's expression only grew more sour, Bryce's gaze and smile flicked to Walt.

He looked tense and livid, and she realized he hadn't been angry yesterday, just hurt. He was angry now, furious even. He nodded at the front door.

"I'll be over in a few minutes."

As polite and soft spoken as his words were, he wasn't asking her to leave—he was telling her. *Okay*, it wasn't like she wanted to hang around with Mama Diaz anyway. Turning toward the door, she felt the lash of Artemesia's displeasure and froze.

"So you've taken to dating livestock. Are you trying to make some point about 'Chelle?"

Bryce spun slowly on her heels, taking a calming breath as she went. She didn't want to be calm. She wanted to draw a lungful of air and tell the little tweaker that the fawning acolytes in her circle might take her attitude, but Artemesia could kiss Bryce's double-wide ass.

And why not tell her exactly that? she thought. But then she saw Walt's face. He looked like he had just been sucker punched in the stomach, his guts spilling out even though the hand delivering the blow belonged to a slip of a woman who probably weighed in at around a hundred and five.

Shaking the stunned look from his face, he shot Artemesia a dark glare and then pivoted. He moved to Bryce, his arm out as he walked. "I'm so sorry, Brycie—"

"A trailer park name if I ever heard one—"

"Enough, Mother." He didn't shout. He didn't need to. The quiet venom coating his voice was enough to shut her up. Reaching Bryce, he wrapped an arm around her shoulder before turning to pierce Artemesia with his sharp stare. "We're going to dinner. You're not welcome here. If you're here when I get back, I'll move again."

He was trembling, his fingertips biting into Bryce's shoulders for a few seconds before he seemed to realize it and relaxed them. "And I don't want to see you at all until you've found some adequate way to apologize to Bryce."

"What in the hell has gotten into you?"

Hearing the surprise in Artemesia's voice, Bryce remembered Erato's warning—*you've never been one of the girls the Perfect Mr. Diaz let mommy chase away.* So was he offering more than the usual fight in the face of Artemesia's disapproval?

Stretching up on tiptoe, Bryce kissed his cheek, grinning at Artemesia's disgusted "Tsk".

"I'll be waiting by the Suburban," Bryce whispered, letting her lips glide over his ear.

Gently, he stopped her. "No, we'll go together...okay?"

She nodded, relieved that the anger clouding his eyes disappeared the instant he looked at her.

"Your father has been spoiling you," Artemesia spat out.

"No, Mother," Walt said, taking his keys from the hook, "he's been spoiling *you*."

He opened the door for Bryce, never once breaking contact with her as they left the apartment and walked to his SUV.

"Wow!" Bryce said as she slid into the Suburban and hooked her seatbelt. "I've read about her, but—wow!"

Walt still held her door open and he studied her with a curious gaze. "How long have you known?"

"At the loft." A little caution had crept in to taint the curious expression and she crafted her explanation with care. "You told me on the patio that your name was actually 'Galtero'. But I didn't really put it together until I saw your signature on the painting. The initials 'DIIG'— 'Galtero Diaz, Junior'." That they were the same initials marking her body in two places made her bring her hand to her chest and his artist's mark.

She didn't want to poke, but the passing caution he had shown worried her. "Why?"

Moving back so that he could shut her door, he gave a little shrug. "We can talk at the restaurant, if you still want," he answered. "Dwelling on Mother and her behavior while I'm driving...well, that has to be an instant recipe for road rage."

Walt shut her door and she fidgeted in her seat, wishing he wanted to talk now. That he hated stick mommy, or at least had some deep issues with the woman, went a long way toward explaining any genuine attraction he felt towards Bryce. Or so she thought—but that was little better than pop psychology. Wasn't it? Frowning, she twisted the charm bracelet until the clasp faced up.

Climbing into the driver's side, Walt saw the attention she was paying to the bracelet. "You need some different jewelry," he groused. "Do you even have any jewelry other than that?"

"Only if watches count," she answered and unclasped the bracelet. She held it out to him, dropping it when he opened his palm in acceptance. "And if you think I need something different, Walt Diaz, you're just going to have to buy it for me."

He smiled, opened the center console and let the bracelet spool into it. "Fair enough."

Bryce watched wordlessly as he put the Suburban in gear and backed from the parking space. His jaw was tense, as if he expected Artemesia to rush from his apartment and throw herself in his path. While the woman might be that desperate, Bryce didn't think she'd be so publicly blatant. No, Artemesia Diaz was much more the closed door type of diva who made sure all the rumors about her stayed rumors.

Bryce remained quiet all the way to the restaurant, unsure if letting him stew over Artemesia's appearance and what the woman had said was a good idea. She half felt the need to sulk, too. But she would be damned if Walt's mother was going to ruin what could possibly be her last night with him.

At the restaurant, he parked the car, seeming to shake off his bad mood in the time it took to walk around to her door and help her out. He held her hand and waited until she had both feet on the ground. "You look really stunning tonight Bryce—I'm sorry if anything was said to make you feel otherwise and that I took so long to say something."

Well, at least she could stop worrying about what Erato had done to her—she only wished she could see it. She glanced down at her legs and feet but still only saw a blurred mess. She thought she was in a two-piece. She could feel the flutter of soft fabric around her arms and ankles while something tighter hugged her hips. But these were just impressions that shifted as she moved.

Letting go of the door, he slid his arm around her waist and bent to nuzzle her neck. "My favorite restaurant, and I know nothing in there is going to compare to your taste." He kissed her throat, the pressure just light enough to keep from bruising her pale skin. "Nothing will be as sweet or creamy." He repeated the kiss, along her jaw line and just below her ear. He ran his lips over hers. "Or as spicy."

Walt drew her tight to him, still holding her hand and pressing his palm against the small of her back. A lovers' dance with no music. She could feel him molding into her curves, feel her nipples beading in response. Far from him making her forget her body, she was aware of every tingling inch of skin, every length of muscle pulled tight in anticipation of where he would touch or kiss her next.

He ran his hand up her back, spreading delicious shivers across her arms and chest. He stopped at the edges of her up do and stroked the wispy strands that refused to be restrained. "You may have ruined all of L.A. for me, Bryce, if I can't keep seeing it with you," he whispered.

Damn, he was dangerous.

"Your lips shouldn't be trembling like you're ready to cry, Brycie."

He was so warm—his voice, his lips, the concerned olive green gaze. Each time they were this close, she could feel her anxiety and resolve melting.

"Kiss me then," she said.

Walt took her mouth with a hard reverence. He swept Bryce up into the kiss. He held her tight around the waist while his other hand pressed against the base of her head, forcing her into a yielding position. His tongue parted her lips, stroking and teasing as if he were kneeling between her spread thighs. She gripped his shoulder to steady herself, the pale, soft silk of her hand a white flag of surrender.

He broke the kiss, his gaze stunned. "I promised to feed you the best Mexican dinner in L.A. tonight."

Standing on tiptoe, she brushed her lips against his before gently nibbling at his ear. "You promised to fuck me, too," she reminded him. "And you didn't really specify in which order."

"Food's closer."

There was no mistaking the heat or reluctance in his voice. The heat, she thought, because he wanted to take her. His need pressed hard against her stomach. But there was still a very good chance Mama Diaz hadn't gotten tired of waiting at his apartment.

She nodded, knowing more than just acquiescence flickered in her gaze.

Walt shut the Suburban's door and guided her into the restaurant, the touch of his hand light between her shoulder blades. The restaurant's entryway seemed dark after their loitering in the parking lot, and she closed her eyes while he talked to the host. After the man said it would be a few more minutes before their table was ready, she felt Walt slide behind her, his mouth at her ear.

"Keep your eyes closed." His fingertips pressed lightly at her shoulders and he turned.

Bryce turned with him, wondering why he seemed to steer her back toward the entrance. If he'd managed a surprise, she would have seen it when they walked in no matter how dark it was. All she'd seen were some velvet cushion chairs and...

A mirror.

"Open them."

Bryce obeyed slowly. The first thing she saw was the reflection of their heads, his lips against her hair. His gaze was sultry, the same sexual heat pouring off him that had marked all their encounters this weekend. But something immense and tender lurked in his gaze, too—something that turned the time they'd spent locked to one another into more than pleasurable fucking.

"Stop looking at me," he growled playfully.

She gave a slow, short shake of her head and mouthed her disobedience. *No.*

"Afraid?"

"I can't help wanting to look at you," she answered and then pouted. "And what do you mean, 'afraid'?"

168

"Of having your world view changed?"

Relenting, she looked at her image in the mirror, expecting more of the same fuzzy rendering she'd seen all night. The urge to cry struck her hard and fast in the chest. Erato's art, however subtle, was here. But the underlying canvas was still clearly her own. Her gaze moved over each element—recognizing how it was different and yet unchanged. Erato had pulled the honey-blonde hair back in a loose Regency bun that suggested a very planned, yet casual, disorder.

The makeup highlighted her pale features. The shadowing around the eyes was smoky and intense, emphasizing the bedroom quality of their hazel coloring. A spot of color flushed each cheek and her lips were a bruised cherry, though Bryce would have wagered that Walt was responsible for their current coloring. The matching top and skirt were a medium teal with gray sequined embroidery. The English-cut bodice flattered her shoulders and gave an elegantly elongated impression of her neckline. The sleeves were georgette and flowed loose and diaphanous, their ends weighted with a double row of the gray sequins. The skirt narrowed until about two inches above her knees. From there, pleated georgette sectioned the last foot of fabric into an airy hankie-hem. The skirt's graceful drop points danced around her ankles and the dark gray silk pumps.

"You look surprised," Walt said. "Almost like you didn't dress yourself."

If you only knew! Bryce thought, suppressing a nervous smile. "Well...ah...the lighting's different in my apartment."

"I think the lighting's been different in your head," he said and kissed her temple. "But that's changing, yes?"

They were quietly interrupted with the news that their table was ready. Instead of the host, a much older gentleman led them back to their table, his manner with Walt warm and familiar. Bryce could feel the curious looks he cast at her as they crossed the restaurant. When they reached the table, he moved to pull Bryce's chair out, but Walt put his hand on the low-backed chair.

"Please, let me."

The old man moved to the side, smiling at Bryce. Walt bent low, his strong arms on either side of her as he gripped the chair seat. He helped her slide the chair into place, his whole aura intimate and possessive. The man pulled the opposite chair out, waving Walt in. He, too, bent low and intimate, his words just barely reaching Bryce's ears.

"Esta es *la senorita?*"

Walt flushed and the skin around his eyes crinkled as he struggled to manage a discreet grin. "Si."

"Ah...you should have made your reservations directly with me!" He raised his hand, summoning a waiter to the table.

He whispered something in the waiter's ear, and the younger man scurried off. A few seconds later, the lighting in their section dimmed. The waiter returned, carrying candles and a vase of Mexican lilies. When the candles were lit, he stepped back to the next table and waited. The old man took Bryce's hand and bowed at the waist.

"Beautiful lady, I am Victor Chavez." He kissed her hand and then motioned to the restaurant. "This little slice of sanity is mine."

All but tongue tied, Bryce could only manage a blush and simple "Thank you".

"Would you," he started, his tone that of a humble admirer, "would you allow me to pick the meal and wine for the evening?"

"Yes, thank you." She nodded, delighted. A week ago his attention would have sent her running from the room, or at least had her desperately wanting to.

Victor bowed again, beaming at Walt before he snapped his fingers and took the waiter with him.

"What did he mean by his question?" Bryce asked, leaning as close across the table as the candles would allow.

Walt chewed his bottom lip, the even top row of his teeth showing. He gave his head a little shake, surprising Bryce at his reluctance to answer.

"Oh, you're not going to get away with a 'no'." She stretched her leg under the table. Sliding the tip of her gray silk pump under the hem of his pants leg, she rubbed just above his ankle.

"You're not very good at torture, love."

His olive green gaze was determined. Bryce arched one brow and withdrew her foot to a safe distance.

"No, put it back."

He may have meant to command her, but there was too much want in his voice. She brought her foot even with his and teased him with a soft nudge. "What did he mean?"

Walt dropped his gaze. His hands fiddled with the cloth napkin. "It's just that he asked a few months ago why I'd started dining alone. I guess he's surprised to see me with a girl."

She pulled her foot back again. "But he didn't say 'a' girl, he said 'the' girl."

Even with the low lights and flickering candles, Bryce could see that he was blushing.

"Yes, 'the' girl."

That was the only admission she was going to get from him, she realized, and she gently slid her foot back under the hem of his pants. Walt placed his palms flat on the table and surreptitiously glanced at the length of the table cloth. It was long enough that the fabric hung an inch over the floor.

"Take off the pump."

This time it was a command. She toed the shoe off and then returned to caressing the bottom swell of his calf. *Yes, better.* The contact and the look in his eyes made her wet. Her breasts were tight, swollen and sharp-tipped.

"I...uh..." She was at a loss for words and couldn't have spoken had she found any.

"Yeah." He reached across the table to hold her hand. His thumb lightly wrestled with hers. "Me, too."

The things he was doing to her hand were driving her crazy. He slid his thick thumb back and forth against the tight webbing between her fingers. His light scratches against her palm promised a night both tender and rough. She felt as if Walt was fucking her in front of the entire restaurant.

He slowed but didn't stop his caresses when Victor approached the table carrying a bottle of wine and two glasses. Victor set the glasses down, showing the label first to Walt and then to Bryce. It was, of course, from the senior Diaz's vineyards.

"God's own wine," Victor said and started working the cork loose. He watched Bryce as he did so. "Did this young man tell you I'm his *Padrino*—his godfather?"

"I hadn't yet," Walt answered.

Victor's expression was forgiving, his gaze dancing with the flicker of candlelight. "Well, lovers think of other things first, yes?"

The exchange nearly floored Bryce. It wasn't merely a restaurant owner with whom Walt was friends, or even an old and dear friend he had told about "the girl". It was his godfather! And Walt had told him long before this weekend and Percy's appearance.

With the cork freed, Victor poured their wine and placed the bottle on the table. "I see there are things you need to talk about," he said, bowing again at Bryce before he left the table.

"I think talking is the last thing on my mind," Walt said with a soft laugh.

Bryce bit at the inside of her cheek. She certainly didn't want to spoil Walt's mood, but she needed to know something, particularly if their relationship was going to extend beyond one breathtaking weekend.

Taking control of his hand, she looked at him, her gaze gentle but probing. "It's not quite the last thing on my mind," she said, choosing her words with the utmost care. "Why were you upset that I figured out who your parents are?"

Chapter Fifteen

Walt let Bryce keep possession of his hand despite his sudden need to pull back. He had hoped he could make her forget, make himself forget, that the "Wicked Witch of the West Coast" was his mother. He had no sense of how to answer her question. Even though he'd never been in love before, he'd never rushed to abandon any of his prior relationships. At least, not with the women he had chosen.

"My parents' marriage was arranged," he explained. "Mother thinks it's perfectly acceptable to arrange my marriage as well—and to block any relationships that might make her plans...obsolete."

"Block?"

Walt took a deep breath before answering. "Well, she has a variety of tactics. Two women, Vivienne and Carita, she bribed with industry contacts—an agent for Vivienne and an exclusive acting coach for Carita." He took another breath and shuffled through his past affairs. "One, Claire, she got into the MBA program at Stanford, with a scholarship. With another, she had the girl's graduate application held up until she agreed not to see me anymore."

Bryce's expression was shocked, angry, sympathetic, and filled with a quarter dozen more emotions he couldn't name. She gave him a comforting smile and squeezed his hand.

"Well, I've just got to turn a paper in tomorrow and my grad degree is done," she said with a wink.

Did that mean she didn't want things to go back to business-as-usual Monday morning? Walt tilted his head and studied her for a second before returning the squeeze. He couldn't read her right now, and it was too much to hope that Artemesia's behavior hadn't solidified Bryce's plans of limiting things to a weekend affair.

But she had admitted the possibility—even the desire—yesterday, hadn't she? If he could convince her he was sincere, that he not only could, but truly *did*, find her beautiful, it wouldn't have to end tomorrow. Artemesia's calling her "livestock", however, hadn't helped.

Walt squeezed her hand again, a little harder than he meant to. "Sorry...I get a little *tight* where Mother's concerned."

The forgiving nod told him she understood. Then came, "What about Chelle?"

Chelle—"Rochelle" on her birth certificate—was still a festering wound. Not because he'd loved her, but because it showed the lengths to which his mother would go.

"Mother's a devout Catholic," he started, wishing Victor would arrive with the food and he could leave his answer to some day far off in the future. "So she says, anyway. She paid for Rochelle's abortion."

Bryce's hand escaped his and she held it over her heart. *Over my mark*, he thought and tried not to reach across the table and take her hand back.

"Y-yours?"

Walt shrugged. "I've always used protection—until you." He brought his hands together on the table and ran the edges of the cloth napkin through them. "Chelle said, one night, after a little too much alcohol, I didn't. Only she decided to announce it when we were at dinner with my parents."

Bryce reached across the table and took both his hands in hers. She looked on the verge of crying and he wondered why. Was it because he might have gotten another woman pregnant or because of what had happened to the baby?

"Mother was dropping sly hints about how *different* Rochelle's background was, letting her know upper-middle class just wasn't good enough for her son."

Bryce released one of his hands and pushed a candle to the side. Reaching up, she cupped the curve of his jaw and ran the pad of her thumb across his bottom lip. The way she touched him, he knew she wouldn't make him continue with the story if he didn't want to. But telling her felt right; he wanted her to know how serious he'd been when they'd made love with chance their only protection against conceiving.

"She broke up with me the next day...told me a week later that she'd had an abortion." He saw a little shudder pass over Bryce and she blinked once, slowly.

"But how do you know your mother would stoop so low?" Bryce asked.

"Mother bragged about it." His voice roughened. "How it had taken her a hundred thousand to prove Rochelle was just white trash, but that it had been worth every penny."

Bryce still cupped his face and he placed his hand over hers before continuing. "I was living in the L.A. compound when she told me. That was mid-December."

And right before he moved into Bryce's apartment building. He watched her expression, worried she'd think that he'd chosen her as a safe rebound. Hell, she was anything but safe. She owned him right now and didn't even realize it. When her gaze only grew warmer, softer, he relaxed. Turning his head, he kissed her palm just as Victor and the waiter approached.

The waiter carried two bowls of *Sopa di Ostiones.* The smell of oysters fried in wine and floating in a mix of tomato, garlic, potatoes and carrots, reached him before the two men did. Bryce retreated to her side of the table, her expression a little nervous.

"Bryce has confessed, *Padrino,*" Walt teased, "that *real* food is virtually unknown to her."

Bryce blushed and looked caught somewhere between relieved and embarrassed. "It's just that, if it didn't come from a can or a box, my mother didn't serve it. But this *does* smell delicious."

Victor rested his hand on Bryce's shoulder, leaning close to her. "For you, my dear, I will make whatever you want. I will send Filo out to find something in a can...but I think, once you taste my oyster soup, you will want to make it for your mother. Show her how it's done, no?"

Bryce smiled, but Walt detected a wince beneath it. Sensing she had an even worse relationship with her parents than he had with his mother, Walt wanted to touch her, comfort her in whatever way she would let him. Instead, he watched her dip her soup spoon into the bowl. Whatever timidity she must have felt, she suppressed it and scooped up one of the larger pieces of oyster.

Victor watched with one hand to his mouth, and Walt guessed his godfather fought the urge to chew his nails until Bryce pronounced the dish a success or failure. She finished her spoonful. This time there was no wince hiding behind the relieved smile.

"This is good," she said, looking up at Victor.

The old man grinned and wagged an indulgent finger at her. "Wait until you taste the calamari steaks!"

Bryce's grin didn't falter, but the instant Victor was out of earshot, she glanced at Walt. "That's...uh...squid, right?"

Seeing the way Bryce's entire face puckered when she said "squid", Walt chuckled. "Yes, but it's just as good—his special brandy sauce is famous in three countries."

She gathered another spoonful of soup, hesitating before she took it into her mouth. "Your godfather, right?"

Walt nodded.

"And you adore him?"

Another nod. Damn, she was cute like this, her pointed question more blatant than she probably realized. "You'll love it," he promised. "*Padrino* or not."

Chapter Sixteen

Walt hesitated, his house keys out but frozen an inch from the deadbolt. "She could still be inside," he cautioned.

Bryce lightly scratched her chin as she thought it over. "If she is, she's likely to bite," Bryce joked. "So, *you* take her wrists and I'll take her ankles."

She could see the tension that had built during the drive back begin to ease from him. He arched one fine black brow at her—the one with the little scar.

"Just how nefarious is your plan?"

"Oh...I thought we'd just sit her on her butt in the middle of the parking lot," Bryce answered. "My aunt used to drag my cousin out into the middle of the front yard when he'd throw a tantrum—said it was too good a show for the neighbors to miss."

"So there's more than just the maiden aunt in your family tree?"

His tone was teasing but his gaze drilled into her. He had tried once or twice this weekend to get her to talk about her family despite being silent on his. Now that he had opened up, was he expecting a little reciprocity?

"Why don't we see what we have to deal with inside before you quiz me on my family?" She followed the suggestion with a smile, though the idea of explaining how and why she broke all contact with her family when she turned eighteen clawed a hole in the lining of her stomach.

"Good point." Adopting a mock S.W.A.T. stance, he asked, "Do you want to go in high, or low?"

"High." No way was she crouching in a skirt.

"Well, I don't know about that, you could take it in the chest."

"I'd rather take it in the bedroom," she shot back. "Plus, she's short—you're more likely to take it in the head going in low."

"Another good point." This time he scratched his chin. "Maybe we should go to your place instead."

Not unless Erato had popped in with a cleaning crew of pixies since the last time. "I'm pretty sure your mother is gone by now, aren't you?"

He shrugged. "Probably, but I've never actually been inside your place."

Bryce took the keys from Walt and unlocked the deadbolt and doorknob. "It's a typical grad student mess, I promise."

"And next week?" He still hesitated on his doorstep.

"The official student handbook says I don't have to clean until the degree is in hand—particularly since I'll be looking for a full-time job." Bryce opened the door since he obviously wasn't going to do it.

Stepping inside, the apartment seemed blissfully Artemesia free. Bryce crossed to the kitchen, peeking in cupboards and drawers. "Nope, not here." She went to the bedroom and opened the door.

"Uhm...did you make your bed after we...uhm...well, you know?" she asked. Walt didn't answer and she looked at him. He still stood just inside the front door. "Scaredy cat," she hissed. "Did you make up your bed?"

He shook his head.

"Ewww." She shuddered and the teal georgette sleeves of her dress fluttered in a ripple from her shoulders to wrists. "That's just not right."

"She's...*erasing*...you." His lips were pressed tight, the upper one all but invisible. His jet black hair had fallen around his face. With the broad, flat length of his nose and darkened green gaze, he looked like a panther.

Like a panther protecting his mate, Bryce thought. A deep thrill worked its way to the surface of her skin and spread out in a wave of goosebumps. She leaned against the bedroom doorframe, half hidden.

"Then let's un-erase me," she challenged and slowly disappeared from view.

As she moved to sit at the foot of the bed, she could hear his approach. Unrushed. Determined. She heard him unbuckle his belt and the sliding "fwip" as he pulled it through the belt loops. The sound was forceful—dangerous from the tension that held him. There was an ecstatic contraction of cunt and nipples, and she moaned the second before he turned the corner and came into view.

The belt was coiled in on itself, and he moved to place it on his dresser. Something must have shown in her hazel gaze because he turned back to her and tossed the belt onto the bed. Bryce licked her lips. When he closed his eyes and mirrored her action, she shivered. Then he opened his eyes and she was sure he could see through her clothing to the hard nipples and wet pussy.

"Take your top off." He held his arms stiff and she could see his tension in the way he clenched and unclenched his hands.

Bryce grabbed the sequined hem and stripped the top away, slowly at first, and then all at once at the sound of his impatient growl. Walt leaned over, almost against Bryce but not touching her as he reached for the belt.

"Hands out, wrists together."

She obeyed, trembling with the need to touch him but waiting for his command to do so. Her readiness surprised her. She'd seen bondage photos before, read a story or two. They'd all left her dry. But now she was drenched with the need to have him dominate her.

Walt looped the belt tightly around her wrists and then firmly stuck a finger between her lips. She opened her mouth when he pushed down, and he stuck part of the belt strap between her teeth so that she effectively was tethered to herself. He slipped out of his shoes and stripped his pants and briefs away. Cock jutting forward, he stepped between her legs and pushed her skirt up high enough that she could spread her legs. Lightly running his fingertip along the back of one of her bound hands, he gave her permission to touch him.

Bryce wrapped her hands around his thick shaft. She began stroking him, her whole body pitched forward with need. He grabbed her head, tilting it back until she looked into his olive green gaze. The strap was tight against her chin and she had to strain to keep her hands around his cock. With his fingers still playing in her bound hair, he took the pins out singly and tossed them on the dresser behind him. She could feel her hair falling feather light around her shoulders. Walt kept one hand knotted in her soft tresses, dropping the other to knead her breasts. He simultaneously explored her nipple and tolerance with pinches that grew harder and longer, while her soft groans begged for more.

He pushed her hands away and forced her to stand, the belt strap still in her mouth. Her forearms grazed her over-stimulated nipples, making it hard for her to stand still. Seeing the source of her distress, he only teased them to harder points. Letting go of her hair, he dropped his head and rapidly flicked the swollen buds with his tongue before he swept each one into his mouth in turn. She squirmed and he moved both hands to her hips. Increasing the pressure of his tongue and lips on her breast, he drew her tighter to him and closer to the edge of orgasm. Her whole body trembled beneath the rough pleasure of his mouth.

She arched against him, pleading with her body for him to end the torture and bring her to climax.

Releasing Bryce at last, he stripped her skirt down, groaning at the sight of the garters and button-sided panties Erato had dressed her in.

"That's just evil," he panted.

She watched him as he bent his knees and tensed his stomach muscles so that the tip of his cock pushed against her panties. Just the thin fabric prevented him from touching her clit. He nuzzled her neck, his fingertips tracing the top edge of the garters before moving down over their straps, front and back. He pushed the fabric of her panties aside and eased the head of his erection between her labia. Tracing the lace edging of the underwear with one hand, he used the other to rub his cock head up and down her clit. Then he pushed further down, teasing the circle of her cunt. Her pussy was a raw slit of need, and she pictured her juices coating his cock and fingers.

"Brycie, you're so wet for me now," he said, running his hand back up to her clit, slickening the throb of flesh with her cream before pushing the hood in small circles. With his free hand, he unbuttoned one side of the panties. He switched hands, dipping back into the pocket of her cunt, teasing the tight circle and then rubbing his cock over her clit again while he unbuttoned the other side.

Removing Bryce's panties, he left her garters, hose and pumps on.

Pressing gently on her shoulders, he had her sitting perched at the edge of the bed. He moved to her side, standing with one foot on the floor and one knee on the mattress. He took the belt from her mouth and pulled her hands over her head, wrapping the belt's end around his fist. His cock was at mouth level and he had her twisting at the torso to suck him in while she kept her pump-clad feet flat on the floor.

He brushed the tip of his wet cock against her mouth, whispering her name when she opened to accept it. She started with small licks, cleaning her honey from the dark shaft, her tongue traveling its length, swirling at the top and the small circle where her juice and his pre-cum mixed. When she took the head into her mouth, she felt the belt strap twist tighter, and Walt pulled her forward, forcing her to take more of his cock.

"Hold your legs open, Brycie," he ordered. She obeyed, knowing that he only had to make a slight turn of his head and her cunt would be on display to him in the dresser mirror. "You said you could get off just with the contractions."

Gawd, the way his cock filled her mouth, slick and hot, she was close to getting off without any other stimuli. Still sucking him, she gave a throaty "Yes", her answer vibrating against his shaft. He swelled bigger, his ass and thighs tensing with restrained pleasure.

"Show me," he ordered.

◨ ◨ ◨

When she moaned against him, Walt almost came. His gaze snapped from the shiny salmon-colored slash of pussy to her cherry red lips as she worked his cock. "Show me," he repeated, cinching her more tightly to him before turning to stare in the mirror.

She slid her ass forward on the mattress until she hovered half off the edge. Tucking her heels beneath the bed's frame, she kept her pussy spread wide. The inner muscles of her thighs trembled with the effort of maintaining the position, and one breast pushed against his leg as she strained to keep her mouth firmly around his shaft.

There, the first contraction, her hole sliding up and almost disappearing between her labia until she relaxed the muscles. She did it again, this time syncing her mouth to the movement of her cunt.

Perfection. Walt sighed. She had given herself over completely, her trust unconditional. He watched her breast jiggle lightly as she sucked him. The marks were still there, where he had claimed her not only for himself but for his children, too. Her strokes and contractions came faster and he locked his gaze on the reflection of her pussy. His mark was there, too, in the exposed fold of her thigh.

Bryce was moaning now, sucking and humming him to the edge of climax as her labia began to flutter and jump. Her exposed nipple was hard, drawn tight so that thick ridges lined the areola. She flexed her ass and thighs now, too, her whole body participating as she breached the threshold of her climax. Fresh cream trickled from her, sliding from her tight pussy and down her perineum to make the bright pucker of her ass glisten with lust.

Walt jerked, coming down her throat. She took him in greedy gulps as she continued to roll the muscles of her ass and perineum. She had him worked up with the beautiful splay of her cunt. He jerked again and knew there was another burst waiting behind the second. Something that had grown hollow without his realizing it filled with each pump of cum into her sweet, accepting mouth.

Spent, he released his grip on the belt and guided her down onto the bed. He took the strap off her wrists and rubbed away the light red band marking her skin.

"You're not afraid I'll run away?" she asked.

"Not when you're so eager to stay tied up." He could feel his confidence shape his smile. "And, as deranged as I'm afraid it might sound—I would have to stalk you if you ran away."

She raked her fingers through his hair and tugged at the roots. He followed the pull, rolling on top of her.

"Like a gorgeous black panther stalking his mate?" she asked.

She was breathing hard and a playful glimmer in her eyes told him she would welcome the chase. He slid down the bed to where her knees were still bent over the edge, her legs loosely closed. He parted them, his knees touching the ground at the same time his lips passed over her naked pussy.

He blew once against the exposed clit in warning. "Or his meal."

🀫 🀫 🀫

Sweet Jesus, he was going down on her again. Bryce felt his tongue spooning and licking the cream from her slick cunt. She was drunk from the pleasure of it, wondering how she could have spent the first eleven years of sexual maturity without the sweet torture of a man's mouth locked to her pussy. But then she'd never met a man like her Walt.

He amplified his assault, sliding into her two fingers wide. He inserted a third finger, flexing them inside her as he stroked deep and laved her clit. She knotted her fingers in the silky black strands of his hair, her thumbs pressed against his temples as she controlled the position of his head. *There was nothing so good,* she thought, moaning and wriggling against his mouth, *as having a man three fingers deep inside you while he sucked and licked at your clit.*

Bryce locked her ankles behind him, felt the firm resistance of his muscled thighs against the heel of her pumps. She moved to kick the shoes off but he caught her leg with his free hand and put her foot back in position.

She teased him with the threat of more pressure from the heels. Drawing her legs tighter, she cinched his mouth to her pussy.

Releasing his hair, she massaged her breasts and hips before she rose into a sitting position. She flung one arm behind her for support, arching her back and pressing the palm of her other hand against the back of Walt's head. His fingers were buried to the knuckles inside her and he kept flexing them, stretching the ring of her cunt wider.

She looked at their locked bodies in the mirror. His was hard, chiseled, the heel of her pumps cupping just below his tight, muscled ass. His shoulders were broad, forcing her legs wide and making her perineum contract so that she was clamped down on the thick triangle of his thrusting fingers. She was soft, lush, her body rolling as she rode his mouth and hand. It was the first time she had ever become aroused from looking at her naked reflection. The sight pushed her over the edge and she curled around him, begging him to keep fucking her while she came.

The force of her climax had Bryce squeezing her eyes shut. She felt the spread of fire leaving her cunt, simultaneously traveling down her thighs and up over her stomach. Her toes and face went numb as he wrenched another climax from her. She was filling his hand with cream, her pussy slurping his fingers back into her. And then it was more than just three fingers in her cunt. He had worked his pinkie in and was halfway down his palm.

He rotated his hand until his thumb was pressed against the quiver of her ass.

"Yes," she moaned, thinking of the thick tip of his thumb invading her netherhole. It would be a delicious prelude to his cock possessing her there. She wiggled against his thumb, trying to relax her muscles enough that they would allow it in. "Yes," she panted again.

Walt pushed into her, his fingers stilling in her cunt while the tip of his thumb pressured the tense ring of her ass into admitting him. Another firestorm spread across her flesh and Bryce tossed her head back. His thumb was completely in her, the rest of his hand stretching her cunt as he was forced to pull out to the wide base of his knuckles. She wanted to grind her way to oblivion, but knew she could easily injure herself in her eagerness.

It's just so damn good, she thought as she collapsed onto the mattress, vision graying as she jerked in climax.

Chapter Seventeen

"Brycie, love, are you okay?"

Walt's voice was tender, concerned, and she could feel him brushing the hair away from her face.

"Brycie, baby, answer me."

Her eyelids fluttered open. "I'm fine—great," she corrected. "I think maybe I passed out."

"Passed out?" More concern, his tone bordering on incredulous. "From what?"

"From you," she sighed and wrapped her arms around his neck. She pulled him to her in a kiss, tasting her own juices. She deepened the kiss, tasting more of herself as she ran her tongue along Walt's and sucked at his lips. "Don't tell me you never made a girl pass out before?" she asked.

"No—another first." He kissed her mouth, nose and forehead before pushing away. "I'll be right back."

Bryce closed her eyes and quickly fell into a light sleep while he was out of the room. She woke to him gently caressing her cheek with the back of his fingers.

Seeing her eyes open, he moved down and unhooked her hose from the garter belt. He rolled the silk hose down her leg, stopping to take the pumps off before continuing. Then he unfastened the garter belt, coaxing her to raise her hips so that he could remove it completely.

"Now," he said. "Up under the covers with you."

"Are you coming with me?" She mumbled the question as she slowly rolled onto her stomach and crawled up the bed. She was bone tired again, the exhaustion claiming her body absolute.

"Just a few heart beats away from joining you," Walt assured her as he pulled the quilt across her.

Blinking, trying to keep awake, she saw him gather their clothes from the floor and fold them into neat piles that he placed on top of his dresser. He left the room and she could hear him double checking that the front door and sliding glass patio door were locked. He turned off the lights in the rest of the apartment, then came back to the bedroom, turned that light off, and joined her in bed. She snuggled with her back to him, his arm around her waist and his lips pressed against her shoulder.

Now all she had to do was write a damn short story and turn it in to Professor Hardy and the world would be perfect.

▨ ▨ ▨

The paper! Bryce's eyelids flew open and she eased herself far enough off the mattress that she could see the alarm clock. It was already a quarter past midnight, and she had a minimum of six thousand words to write and turn in by two p.m.

She rolled over and lightly shook Walt. He compressed at her touch and tried to nestle deeper between the soft cushion of her body and the mattress. His hand cupped her bottom, drawing them closer together.

"I've got to go for a bit," she said, stroking the edge of his mouth. "My paper, remember?"

His face turned into her touch, his mumble sounding something like "s'not Muhnday".

"But it is Monday." She didn't want to shake him too hard. "I'll call around seven—let you know how far along I am, okay?"

His "kay" was just as mumbled, and she gently slid from his embrace and tucked the covers around him. She slipped her top and skirt on, hugging the shoes and the rest of the clothing against her chest. At the door, she grabbed her keys and then debated whether she should take his to lock his deadbolt. It was after midnight, so the gated entry to the courtyard would be locked. She wouldn't finish the paper before he woke—would be lucky to crank out the minimum six thousand words in time and proof it. No, she wouldn't need them. Locking the bottom lock and pulling the door shut behind her, she left his keys on the hook.

Standing in front of her door, she saw light seeping underneath. She opened the door, expecting to see only

Erato, but finding Percy with her as well. Percy pounced forward and pulled Bryce to the center of the room.

"You're going back, yes?" she asked, her words even more rapid-fire than at the start of this whole adventure.

"Yes." Bryce answered. She felt waspish—clothes wrinkled, her hair and makeup undoubtedly a mess; she looked nothing at all like the junior muse with all her haute couture splendor. Of course, Percy probably hadn't spent the night being thoroughly loved, either. "Not that it's any of your business, Percy."

"But it is!" Percy clapped and spun to face Erato. "So?"

"Fine," Erato sighed. "Your transfer is approved pending the results on the final paper." She pointed at the monitor, and the computer and screen blipped to life.

"I don't get this," Bryce said. She looked to Erato for answers. They'd exchanged enough intimate moments over the weekend, so surely the woman would provide an explanation.

"I told you," Erato said. "Percy wants to work for me—immediately after I learned she'd stuck you with an old sheet and a charm bracelet, I tracked her down."

Bryce moved to the couch and sank into its overstuffed cushions. "Go on."

"Since I wouldn't give her a chance to prove herself, she created her own—you."

"My short story?" Bryce asked. "It's not even started yet."

Erato shook her head. Percy bounced in the desk chair.

"Walt's painting?"

Percy giggled. "Noooooooooo. You are so cold." Another clap. "Try again!"

"Enough," Erato told her new assistant. She looked back at Bryce. "A metadrama."

"Drama within drama, drama about drama...words feeding images and so on?" Bryce asked.

"Ooooh, she's got a brain," Percy chirped, her bouncing only intensifying.

"Drop the sarcasm, Percy," Erato warned.

More than just a little confused, Bryce tilted her head and studied Erato's sincerity. "But then whose metadrama am I?"

"Yours, dear."

"And the toga and bracelet?" *Those had to have been real, right?*

"Stage props," Percy chimed in.

Bryce's gut felt hollowed out and her mouth began to tremble. "And Walt?"

"Great improvisation!" Percy collapsed against the back of the office chair in a fake swoon. "Holy Zeus, he's hot."

Bryce looked at Erato, her expression demanding a better explanation.

"All yours, darling." Erato answered. With her first three fingers splayed, pinkie and thumb joined in a circle, she placed her hand over her heart. "Muse's honor, and all."

"I still don't get all of it—metadramas don't really work like that," Bryce said, most of the tension leaving her body at the realization that the only magic worked on Walt had originated solely with her.

Erato pointed to where Percy was sitting. "Plant your ass in that chair for the next twelve hours, honey. You'll have it all figured out by then."

With that, both muses were gone.

▩ ▩ ▩

Leaving the pumps and undergarments on the couch, Bryce sat down in the office chair. The screen was just as blank as she had left it on Friday. She flipped through her syllabus to the sample cover sheet and began typing in the class details and her student information. There was a sharp rap at the door.

Bryce turned her head and stared at the door for a second. It was nearing one, too late for real visitors and she wouldn't expect Walt to knock like that. If Percy was back for another round, why the formality? Bryce went to the door and opened it, her expression neutral in case it was Walt and not the renegade muse.

Artemesia Diaz was sliding the antenna down on her cell phone and dropping it back into her purse. Taking advantage of Bryce's shock, she pushed into the room, pivoted and locked the door. Bryce suppressed a growl, half irritated with herself for letting two much smaller women force their way into her apartment over the course of just a few days. Although Artemesia shouldn't have made it past the gate securing the courtyard.

"We have business to discuss." Artemesia's words came out in a cut fashion, seeming to drip with the same precision with which she planned on excising Bryce from Walt's life.

"The only thing we have to discuss is how you're leaving my apartment," Bryce replied evenly. "Nicely, on your own, or—"

"Don't presume to threaten me, you oversized gold digger." She pulled a pocket book from her purse, flicking it open as she walked toward the couch. "I've dealt with dozens of girls like you, believe me. And you'll note, none of them are around anymore." Seeing the garter and lingerie panties on the couch, she stopped cold. "I see you're a slut, as well."

Trying to keep the heat of her temper in check, Bryce walked slowly to her phone. She picked the handset up and held it in front of her. "The only thing I was threatening you with was a call to the police—you're trespassing."

Pinching one of the couch's throw pillows by its corner, Artemesia used it to plow the shoes and clothing onto the floor. She sat down on the couch, stepping and twisting on the garter and underwear as she took her seat. Her face was a taut mix of anger and distaste.

"You're not going to call the cops, Bryce," Artemesia assured her. "What was it Mrs. Gretz said when I asked her to call me once you were done rutting and back in your apartment? Ah, I remember...she wanted to know what that 'timid cow' was doing with my beautiful boy." Her eyes swept mercilessly over Bryce's form. "It was difficult to even begin formulating an answer—you're so much worse than anything he's ever brought home before."

Removing a silver pen from the spine of her pocket book, Artemesia started writing the date in slim, looping numbers. "Of course," she started, and shot a glance at the wrecked garter, "even when I realized what the answer was, I still was at a loss to explain it to her in polite terms. He's normally not the kind of man to find even a moment's attraction for a woman so..." Artemesia gestured up and down Bryce's body with her hand. "...a woman so physically *base* that she's willing to do anything in bed to attract a man."

Moving to the payee field of the check, she printed Bryce's name in huge block letters. Big, shapeless letters. Bryce felt her grip on the handset tighten. The plastic creaked from the pressure on it and she placed it back on the cradle. She wouldn't call the cops—unless she had a dead body to report. It wasn't timidity that stayed her, but the desire to handle Artemesia on her own. She was going to have to learn how sooner or later if she planned on making a future with Walt.

Passing by the couch, she went to her desk and began shutting down her laptop so that she could put it in the case. She would play Artemesia's game the same way Walt had, she'd leave the woman fuming in an empty room.

"That is why, isn't it?" Artemesia asked, her tone sweetly mocking despite the obscene slurs. "I bet you like a man in your mouth, filling that little pig snout and greedy gut—you pork it down, don't you?"

Oh, she was good. Bryce would give her that. Had this conversation occurred Friday afternoon, Bryce might have fled her apartment instantly to avoid the confrontation. But a lot had happened since Friday. She'd fallen in love—and through some kind of weird, fucked up osmosis, she saw herself through her lover's eyes. Bryce the Beautiful.

Bryce turned, offering Artemesia a rounded smile that she threw her whole body into. "He's got such a lovely cock," she answered. She licked her lips, leaving them wet and shiny. "Your sense of aesthetics in leaving him uncut..." She stopped, licked her lips again, as if she were remembering the slide of him in her mouth. "...well, just perfect. The fit, the glide."

Artemesia turned red, her face apoplectic from the taunts Bryce fed her. A perverse desire to goad the woman into a stroke surfaced, shimmering for an instant in Bryce's mind before she pushed it back down. Shouldering the computer case strap, she walked toward her bedroom. She'd get a change of clothes. The night manager at the convenience store knew her well enough to let her change in the bathroom.

"You're not walking out on me!" Artemesia screamed. She got up from the couch, following after Bryce as she furiously scribbled numbers and words on the amount lines of the check. "What, you think being a crass little cow is going to drive my offer price up? Believe me when I say I know the cost of a woman like *you*."

Bryce turned in her doorway and stared down at the stick figure that was Walt's *Mother*. "Well, I know it's a hundred thousand to kill a baby—if there actually was a baby. Is killing true love worth more or less?"

Artemesia's skin purpled. The way the air left the older woman's mouth reminded Bryce of a dying goldfish on the linoleum, the glass shards and turquoise stones of its world around it in ruins. Artemesia turned, ripped the check from her pocket book and slammed it down on the coffee table. The force knocked over a new bottle of perfume that Bryce hadn't noticed before. Even with Artemesia winding her tighter by the second, Bryce smiled at Erato or Percy's last bit of humor as she recognized the almost egg-shaped bottle of Joop! Muse.

"I guess true love isn't worth anything more than a cheap perfume." Artemesia snarled the words as she picked up the bottle. Like a pitcher on a mound, her small hand fisted around the glass and plastic.

Bryce stepped back, her shoulder hitting the doorframe and slowing her until it was too late to duck into the bedroom. Artemesia pulled her arm back and then fast-balled the bottle straight at Bryce's head. Bryce pulled left. The bottle's gold colored shell splintered against the wood door frame less than two inches from her ear. The sound was followed almost instantly by the shattering of the clear inner glass. She felt a thick slice cut into the skin of her neck and then the sharp sting of the perfume as it took the same path.

Bryce let the computer bag slide to the floor as she walked swiftly toward Artemesia. She didn't care how Artemesia's antics played with the staff or Walt's earlier lovers, the woman was certifiably insane. As insane as she was, Artemesia still didn't come close to Bryce's own parents. What could she say that Bryce hadn't already heard spilling from the mouth of her mother or stepfather? That she was a fat, lazy cunt? Stupid and utterly unlovable?

Been there, done that a dozen times a day.

"You're going to have to try harder," Bryce snarled.

Artemesia was at the front door by the time Bryce rounded the couch. The woman fumbled to unlock it and appear unconcerned at the same time. Bryce gave a low warning growl, a guttural promise that she couldn't be held responsible for what happened if Artemesia didn't haul her skinny little ass across the threshold in time.

"Damn, she's fast," Bryce said, catching the door on its inward swing as Artemesia shot through it and out onto the sidewalk. Bryce slammed the door, securing each lock with as much of the force trembling through her as she dared to release.

Her neck stung and she put her hand up to the cut. She didn't have to look at her hand to know she was bleeding—the liquid coating her fingers was too viscous to be perfume. She went straight to the bathroom, slamming that door shut, too.

Seeing the trail of red dangerously close to the edge of the blouse's fabric, Bryce grabbed a wad of toilet paper and mopped the blood from her skin. She pressed a second wad gently beneath the cut area while she ran cold water and found her tweezers. A piece of glass, about a quarter inch thick, stuck from her neck.

Bryce secured the exposed portion of glass between the tweezers' ends and pulled slowly, afraid that some of it would break off if she jerked it out the way she wanted to. It was unnerving, feeling the sharp slice of glass exiting her skin, and she gave a jittery growl throughout the length of its journey.

There was more blood with the glass removed. She cleaned the wound and applied pressure until she was sure she could slip out of the blouse without staining it. She needed a shower. A spritz or two of the perfume, with its tantalizing mix of heliotrope and white musk was wonderful. A bottle's worth of it on her skin was rank and eye watering. Briefly, she wondered if Erato was still observing; Artemesia's psychosis was fodder enough to inspire a dozen books. Not that Bryce needed a word more than six thousand.

She clicked the bathroom fan on to clear the fumes at the same time she shut the sink's faucet off. In the shower, she moved quickly through cleaning herself and the cut again, irritated at the loss of time in getting started on her story. Out of the shower, she tossed on a robe and turned the air conditioner to a cooler setting before she scooped up the computer case and headed back to her desk with it.

She pulled the laptop from the case, booting it up while she pulled out the power cord and mouse and plugged those in. She opened Word and checked over her cover page. She still needed a title. Well, that could wait for the end, right? A story didn't have to have a title to start—at least she didn't think it was a prerequisite.

Inserting a hard page break, Bryce faced a blank page once again. She didn't have to start at the beginning. She knew that, too. But it seemed as good a place as any.

Chapter Eighteen

Bryce checked the time in the corner of her computer screen. Eleven thirty a.m. Erato had been close; Bryce had spent almost twelve hours with her ass planted in the chair. But, instead of producing the minimum six thousand words she'd needed, she'd had to go back and shave off five hundred words to avoid going over the seventy-five hundred word ceiling. And now she needed to get the sucker printed out, wake up Walt and beg him to drive her to class since she wouldn't be dressed in time to catch the bus and make it there by two p.m.

Hitting the print button, she waited for the machine to make its little start up noises and then she dashed into the bedroom, careful to avoid the glass and perfume she hadn't had time to clean up. The champagne-colored skirt outfit and the black georgette pants and blouse appeared to have been dry-cleaned. She took the black pants from the hanger and paired it with the blue linen blouse she always wore when trying to present a professional appearance. She grabbed the bulky black jacket she usually hid the blue linen blouse in, gave it a second look and then let it drop to the floor. She'd take it to a charity store later in the week, along with half her closet. Sifting through her dresser, she gave a displeased grunt. Her entire panty drawer, she told herself, was headed straight for the dumpster.

Under and outer garments in hand, she skirted the broken glass a second time and changed in the bathroom—adding just a hint of makeup and tying back her unruly hair. Stepping into a pair of black silk pumps with low heels, she heard the last printed page slide into the catch tray.

As she stepped into the front room, the small rectangle of paper on the coffee table caught her attention. *Artemesia's check!* She scooped the bank draft up as she passed and tore it into little shreds without looking at it. Then she pulled the story from the printer and thumbed through it, checking the page numbering at the bottom and the first and last sentence of each page to make sure nothing was missing. Satisfied, she grabbed her house keys from the hook, snatched up her purse and headed for Walt's apartment.

He didn't answer on the first set of knocks, or the second, even though she called out to him. On the third, she gave a little pound with the heel of her hand. She heard the locks turn and then the door drifted inward as Walt walked to the couch and sat down.

"What do you want, Bryce?"

There was a touch of Mama Diaz in his tone and it took Bryce a second to respond. "Why wouldn't you open the door?"

The coffee table was back in front of the couch and a glass filled with ice sat alongside the bottle of Courvoisier. Bryce frowned. If he was an afternoon drinker, he wouldn't have made it through this past weekend with just the two drinks. She looked at his face and saw a mix of Saturday's hurt and the almost violent anger he had displayed around his mother last night.

She repeated the question. "Why didn't you open the door—you heard me knocking."

He was chewing on his lip—nothing sensual in the act as he apparently sought to control his anger. Reaching for the bottle, he filled the glass but didn't touch it. "It's Monday, right?"

He took the glass, rested it on the arm of the couch and stared through its dark amber filter. Whatever answer he was looking for, she was pretty sure it wasn't at the bottom of the glass.

"What's that got to do with it?" She had rolled her paper into a tube and was flicking it against her thigh.

Walt's grip on the drink tightened, his whole face corkscrewing with an injured wrath. "Answer one of my questions, Bryce. Why weren't you in my bed this morning?"

"I told you last night, at midnight—"

"Right, that it was Monday." He met her gaze but only for an instant. "Didn't sound like 'so long, thanks for the sex but I still think you're a shallow fuck, Walt'." He brought the glass to his lips, hesitating a second before he put it back down untouched. "But I guess that's what it was."

"I woke you and told you I had to finish my paper." She spoke through clenched teeth, her grip on the rolled up story so tight she crinkled the paper. "It's due at two, and, if I don't turn it in, I don't graduate this semester."

"So you need a ride, that's why you came back."

"Yes...I mean—no, that's not it at—"

He smiled at her, as if he'd just caught her in a lie. One more woman in a long line of women who'd lied to him, starting with his mother. "You said you just had to tweak it."

Correction, he *had* caught her in a lie, only it was Saturday's lie. But she wasn't about to admit it. How could she? "What I had was crap, I wrote a new one, about us. I meant to call you at seven, but I got caught up."

Walt gave a little non-committal grunt and reached for the glass of Courvoisier again.

"Damnit, why's it so hard for you to believe me?" She looked through the patio's sliding glass door. "Hell, your easel is still on the patio from Friday afternoon, don't tell me you don't occasionally get caught up?"

He looked at the easel for a second before turning his dark gaze on her. "I think, the difference is, Bryce, that I got caught up in you." He shook his head, his expression reluctant but determined. "Not that it matters now. I don't want to hear your excuses, Bryce. I hope the story means a lot to you."

"It *did* mean a lot to me," she shot back. "I said it was about us—now I guess it's just about a grade."

She tossed the tube of paper at the floor in front of him, the individual sheaves scattering when the roll hit the coffee table. She had the door halfway open and was stepping through it when his cold voice cut in front of her, blocking the way out.

"Why'd you take the check, Brycie?"

Her body refused to turn back to him, allowing only a stunned glance over her shoulder. He wasn't joking, the hurt in his eyes burned bright. "What do you mean?"

"I know Mother was in your apartment, I know she gave you a check for a hundred and fifty thousand dollars."

"I didn't take it." Her heart thumped wildly in her chest. He thought she'd accepted that bitch's bribe? "Why do you think I did?"

"I woke up a little while after you left, you weren't here." He took his first drink of the alcohol. "I heard shouting. By the time I was to my front door, she was outside your apartment—gloating."

He did think she'd taken the money! She could see it in his expression, in the way his mouth trembled as he swallowed another mouthful of the Courvoisier.

"She showed me the checkbook...offered to dump her purse out." He refilled the glass, twisting it in his hands as he refused to look at her. "What did she say? 'Dear girl certainly didn't tear it up and throw the pieces in my face.' And when I knocked on your door—banged on the damn thing, you wouldn't answer."

Bryce thought back to last night. She'd been in the bathroom by then, pulling glass from her throat and running water. "You don't understand—"

"You're right, Bryce, I don't understand!" He slammed the glass down, amber fire sloshing over the rim and wetting his hand. "With Chelle, there was only this big 'what if?' What if she'd really been carrying my child? I'd never contemplated the possibility of sharing something like that with her."

He shoved the coffee table away with his foot and twisted on the couch until he was staring hard at her. "You, Brycie, I wanted that with you—or at least with the person I thought you were."

She was crying, she could feel the hot tears running down her cheeks, smearing her mascara into black streaks of heartbreak. "Your mother..." she started, trying to keep her voice even despite the pain. If anyone had the right to be disillusioned, it was her. "Your mother, barged into my apartment, slammed that damn check down and then broke a bottle of perfume half an inch from my head."

She whipped the door the rest of the way open and ripped the bandage from her throat. She felt fresh blood weep from the edges of the scab as she flung the bandage behind her. "When you were knocking on my door last night, I was in the shower, cleaning off the blood and perfume."

Stepping outside, she grabbed the door, her hand wrenching the knob. "And I didn't rip that goddamn check up until this morning when I realized it was still there. I didn't know how much it was—nor did I *fucking* care."

With that, Bryce slammed the door shut, stalked across the courtyard and out the entry gate. Tears blinding her, she stumbled to the sidewalk and headed east.

☒ ☒ ☒

Walt stared at the door for a few minutes, wondering whether he should chase after her. If she was telling the truth, he'd just made the biggest mistake of his entire life. He started to stand up and his foot brushed against one of the pages she had thrown at him. He scooped the pages up, put them back in order and then placed them neatly on the coffee table. As he pulled the coffee table back into place, he glanced over the cover page, the title catching and holding his attention.

The Reluctant Muse.

Turning to the first page of the story, he started reading. At the end of the first page, he glanced at the clock and then at the cover page again. The turn in date and time, as well as the location and professor, were typed in a tight block at the top right hand of the page. He looked at the clock again—twelve thirty.

Shit. Even if he'd been all smiles and sunshine when she'd shown up, getting her to campus during the afternoon rush hour would have been a feat. He jumped up, took the stack of paper and grabbed his keys. He knocked on her door at the same time he locked his. Was she even inside? He hadn't heard her door slam. Walt knocked a little louder, calling to her, and then he gave up and ran through the gate.

It was less than twenty miles to campus but twenty miles could take three hours on the wrong day in L.A. After parking and finding the right building, he ran up to the classroom door with less than three minutes left. Students were already filing out, clutching slips of paper bearing a blue date stamp in their hands.

Nervously tracing the edge of the paper, Walt waited until the last student had left.

"You're not one of mine," the man behind the desk said.

Walt glanced at the cover sheet to Bryce's story. "Uhm...no, Professor Hardy, this is Bryce Schoene's paper. She...uhm...couldn't bring it herself—is that okay?"

"As long as you're here on time and," he stopped and checked the clock. Less than a minute remained. "And you are."

Taking the pages from Walt, Hardy folded the bottom quarter of the cover sheet where the student information and title were repeated. He ran his nail along the seam he had created and then tore the section loose and stamped and initialed it. He handed the slip to Walt, who put it in his wallet.

Hardy pursed his lips and studied Walt for a second. "Was there something else, young man?"

"It's just, well," he glanced at the polished tile flooring, bewildered at the blush he felt spreading across his face. And the need tightening in his chest. He didn't doubt that he loved Bryce—the paper might tell him whether she loved him, too. "I didn't get to finish reading it."

"I suppose if she trusted you to deliver it..." Hardy started and pushed the paper back across the desk. "But you've only got until a quarter to three, I'm not driving on the Four-Oh-Five any later than three."

Grinning, Walt took the paper and sat down at the nearest desk, quickly re-reading the first page as Hardy opened a grade book and started checking off names while he shuffled through the papers.

Chapter Nineteen

Bryce sat at a sidewalk table at an outdoor café a few blocks from her apartment building. She hadn't gone home yet, wasn't sure if she would until evening. It would be easier then, the courtyard darker. He might not, if he was looking, catch her sneaking in. If he did, the shadows might keep her hurt hidden behind the brave words she'd practiced on her tear-filled walk around the neighborhood. For now, she held a newspaper in one hand and a red felt-tipped pen in the other. The paper was open to the classifieds section and she had already drawn three big circles on the page.

The waiter came over to her table and she tried to wave him off. When he wouldn't leave, she looked up at him. His face a study in disinterest, he slid a slip of paper onto the table.

"Gentleman left this for you."

He had placed the paper face down and she flipped it over as the waiter walked away. It was a blue date stamp with the initials 'T.H.' in small script. To the right of that were her name and the title of the story she had written.

Wadding the paper into a tight ball, she flicked it off the table. *So the jerk had turned her paper in. So what? He was still a jerk—and a chicken, apparently. Leaving the date stamp with the waiter and running off.*

Bryce picked the newspaper back up and gave it a sharp snap. She continued scanning the column and started to circle another brief ad. "Learn Japanese culture while teaching English!"

"That's a little extreme, don't you think?"

At the sound of Walt's voice over her shoulder, Bryce dropped the pen, the circle unclosed. He bent down, brushing against her and filling her nostrils with his scent. Almonds and guava. Seeing the golden brown patch of skin on his neck, she wanted to lean down and lick it but kept both hands on the paper, ignoring him when he tried to return the pen to her. It didn't matter that he had turned her story in, or that he hadn't just given the slip to the waiter and run off. In fact, he was even more of a chicken, having hidden to see what her reaction would be.

Walt placed the pen on the table and went searching for the grade stamp she'd thrown away. Finding it, he came back to the table and sat down. He smoothed the wrinkles out of it while he waited for her to say something.

"I mean—even as mad as I was at my mom, I only moved across town," he said after another minute had passed without her acknowledging him.

Her gaze flicked up and over him before she took the pen, finished the last circle and made another one a few ads down. *Chicken.* "I'm not mad," she said, a sharp smile cutting across her face. *Chicken, chicken, chicken.* "I just don't want to be on the same continent as you are."

"Brycie—"

"Don't. Call. Me. That." She said each word separately, with a full stop. The newspaper trembled in her hands, the bottom edge threatening to rip from the stress of her tight grip.

"Bryce, couples have arguments—huge ones, sometimes."

She stared at him. The muscles around her eyes felt so tense she was sure her gaze could scratch diamonds. It didn't seem to faze him.

"But one of them usually doesn't pick up and move to another country."

"We aren't—weren't a couple." Picking up the pen and date stamp, she shoved them in her pocket and folded the newspaper.

"Yes, Brycie, we were—we are," he corrected, clearing his throat before he placed a restraining hand on her arm. "I know we've only had a short time together, and that I said some terrible things." He fidgeted with the edge of her sleeve, gripping the fabric but not otherwise touching her. "I believed some terrible things, that's the worst of it."

She wanted to nod, to agree that it truly had been the worst of it, but she forced herself to remain cold and distant.

"I read your story," he said, his fingertips daring to touch the back of her hand. "It was weird, having to read it with Hardy there, knowing that he would soon be reading it."

Bryce pulled her hand away and dropped it to her lap where it twisted wildly against its mate. Before the fight this morning, she'd certainly hoped he would read it at some point. Now it just felt like he'd pried open some window on her soul, reading her secrets without revealing any of his own.

"In some parts of the story, it was like you had read my mind," he said. "Like when we were in the loft."

The top button of her blouse was undone, the spread of her collar starting just above the spot where he had placed his artist's mark. She could feel the fabric, feel its flutter as if Walt were drawing the mark all over again.

"I really did think those things when I was drawing on you." He paused, a layer of moisture making his olive green gaze shine bright. "And I don't know how, with your being in my head like that, you can be so sure that you have an exclusive license on insecurity."

Bryce stiffened and pushed away from the table, the chair's metal legs scraping across the concrete sidewalk.

"Brycie, please."

He was holding her there with just his voice and those two words. She brushed an angry hand across her cheek, erasing a tear almost before it had escaped.

Walt reached into his pants pocket, palming something before he put his hand on the center of the table. "I know, I really, really know how hard you had to fight your fear to trust me, and how it must have torn at you this morning when I couldn't offer you the same trust."

She put one hand on the chair's arm, ready to rise and walk out forever. It was, she thought, worse that he understood—and that he understood too late. Walt jumped up before she could leave, swiftly circling the table and dropping to one knee in front of her. He turned his closed fist palm up and slowly opened it to reveal the bracelet with its dove done in mother-of-pearl. Next to the dove was an ivory swan.

Unhooking the clasp, Walt threaded it between her arm and the chair she still clutched. Securing the bracelet around her wrist, he gently grabbed both of her arms just above the bend of her elbows. He looked, for an instant, like he wanted to shake some sense into her, but then he smoothed his palms along the side of her arms. Taking hold of her shoulders, he stretched up and placed his cheek against hers.

"I can't promise you that I won't ever be that stupid again," he said, kissing where his cheek had brushed against hers. "But I love you, and I'll do everything I can to erase the hurt I caused you this morning." He brushed against her other cheek, following it with another kiss. "Everything but let you leave without a fight."

He dropped his head, an errant knight awaiting his queen's sentence. Bryce stared at the black crown of hair with its hidden network of silver highlights. She felt the tremble running through his body at the idea that she would send him away no matter what he said.

It was tempting. Just shut him out, pack up and run. She'd done that before, eleven years ago. She had slipped out of the house in the middle of the afternoon while her parents were out drinking. She'd left with no more than a few hundred dollars, a duffel bag slung over her shoulder and a friend's address out in California—someplace her family would never go searching for her if they even noticed she was gone. That had been liberating. She'd been brave then. Running this time didn't feel brave. This time, the thought of it squeezed at her chest until she was sure she would pass out.

Shrugging from his loose hold on her shoulder, she tucked a strand of hair behind his ear, the swan and dove charms of her bracelet brushing against his skin. He didn't look up and his body only trembled harder.

"Walt," she whispered his name, the single word an exculpation. "I want to go home—back to your place, I mean."

She swallowed hard, the blood freezing in her chest until he finally looked up at her, a relieved smile breaking across his face. He twined his hands in her hair and pulled her down to him in a kiss that felt like forever, but lasted only a few seconds.

"Yes, Brycie, let's go home."

About the Author

Ann Vremont is a mother, wife, licensed attorney, technical writer, high school dropout and former Russian linguist for Army SigInt. She's called Bingo for a living, waitressed at a strip club, scooped ice cream and conducted political surveys—including for the wrong party. She maintains that, if she hadn't dropped out of high school, she would probably be a mineralogist or a geophysicist. Ann further maintains that if she had never met her husband of seventeen-plus years or had their son when she did, she would probably be making her living illegally—or, if unsuccessful, sitting in jail.

She has a large collection of minerals and a growing collection of lighthouses. Having been born and partially raised in Arizona, the mineral collection doesn't surprise her, but she's still puzzling the source of her lighthouse fetish. You can find her on the web at http://www.annvremont.com.

FLY AWAY

Discover the Talons Series

5 STEAMY NEW PARANORMAL ROMANCES
TO HOOK YOU IN

Kiss Me Deadly, by Shannon Stacey
King of Prey, by Mandy M. Roth
Firebird, by Jaycee Clark
Caged Desire, by Sydney Somers
Seize the Hunter, by Michelle M. Pillow

AVAILABLE IN EBOOK—COMING SOON IN PRINT!

Samhain
Publishing ltd.

WWW.SAMHAINPUBLISHING.COM

GET IT NOW

MyBookStoreAndMore.com
GREAT EBOOKS, GREAT DEALS . . . AND MORE!

Don't wait to run to the bookstore down the street, or
waste time shopping online at one of the "big boys." Now,
all your favorite Samhain authors are all in one place—at
MyBookStoreAndMore.com. Stop by today and discover
great deals on Samhain—and a whole lot more!

WWW.SAMHAINPUBLISHING.COM